Printed in the United States of America

First Paperback Edition, June 2016

1 3 5 7 9 10 8 6 4 2

FAC-029261-16134

Library of Congress Control Number: 2015956570

ISBN 978-1-4847-4992-0

For more Disney Press fun, visit www.disneybooks.com

SUSTAINABLE
FORESTRY
INITIATIVE
Certified Chain of Custody
Promoting Sustainable Forestry
www.sfiprogram.org
SFI-01054
The SFI label applies to the text stock

PETE'S DRAGON

By Landry Q. Walker

Based on the Screenplay by David Lowery & Toby Halbrooks

Based on the 1977 motion picture screenplay by Malcolm Marmorstein

Produced by Jim Whitaker

Directed by David Lowery

 PRESS

Los Angeles • New York

CHAPTER ONE

Dark green trees stretched for miles in front of Pete's family car. They were beautiful, towering pines that swayed gently in the breeze. The sun sat low on the horizon, and faint washes of orange and pink peered over the tree line, as if the last touches of daylight wanted to say good-bye. Only the empty road broke the scenic display. It was a narrow two-lane band of asphalt sandwiched between two massive walls of forest. The sight was both amazing and breathtaking.

Not that Pete was paying attention to any of it. Not really. In the backseat of his parents' station wagon, the five-year-old boy focused all of his attention on an oversized storybook sitting comfortably in his lap.

"'This . . . is . . . the . . . story . . . of . . .'"

Pete traced the letters with his fingertips. He had just begun learning to read, and it was sometimes hard for him to sound out the words.

"'. . . a lit . . . little puh . . . puppy,'" Pete continued. "'His nnname is . . . Elll . . .'"

Pete's mother looked back from the front seat. "Elliot," she said encouragingly.

"'Elliot,'" Pete repeated. He gazed at the sentence with the intense type of focus only a child can have. Suddenly, it all snapped into place: "'His name is Elliot!'"

Pete's mother smiled. "You got it!"

Pete grinned proudly. He kept reading. "'He . . . is . . . going . . . on . . . an . . . add . . . veen . . . turr . . . eee.'"

This word was new. Pete mouthed the sounds silently to himself. But it didn't help. He had no idea what an "add . . . veen . . . turr . . . eee" was.

He pointed at the strange word, looking to his mother for help. "What's that?"

"An adventure? You don't know what an adventure is?" Pete's mother asked.

"It's what we're on right now!" Pete's dad said from the driver's seat. "Out here in the wild, not another soul in sight for hundreds of miles, no running water, with only the stars to guide us!"

Pete frowned.

"Is it scary?" he asked quietly.

"Well," his father said with a mischievous smile, "that's the other thing about adventures: you've gotta be brave. Are you brave?"

Pete paused. He hadn't ever thought about whether or not he was brave.

His mother jumped in.

"Of course you're brave," she said, giving Pete a loving smile. "You're the bravest boy I've ever met."

The last light of the sun had faded by then. The blue sky deepened quickly into indigo, and every trace of warmth faded behind the tops of the towering forest. Pete's father reached for the radio, turning the knobs and searching for some music.

"It's getting dark," Pete's mom said. "Let's finish reading later."

Pete closed the storybook and slid it into his backpack, but he couldn't get the zipper to close. He tugged at it. The stubborn zipper still refused to budge.

Pete's mother reached for the backpack. "Here, let me help you with that. . . ."

As Pete's mother worked at the troublesome zipper, a glimmer of light caught the young boy's attention. "A star!" he exclaimed, pointing up at the sky through the car window.

His mother looked up. "That's the North Star. It's there to guide your way."

Pete cocked his head to the side, thinking aloud. "On an adventure?"

"Exactly!" she replied.

Pete grinned and stared up at the star. Maybe his mom was right. Maybe the star was guiding them on an adventure right now!

What happened next, Pete would never clearly recall. A deer suddenly bounded into the road, and his father slammed on the brakes. The car's tires screeched as they skidded across the road, and the vehicle spun out of control. Suddenly, the world tipped, and all Pete could see was a blur of dirt and branches and tree trunks. He slammed into the side of the car and banged his head. Hard. Then everything went dark.

CHAPTER TWO

The deer dashed quickly away, disappearing into the night. The road through the forest was empty once more.

A trail of wreckage lay scattered across the damp grass, leading to where the family's station wagon had crashed into a tree trunk. Not far away, barely visible in the darkness, lay the oversized storybook. The wind picked up, and the pages began to turn. Pete's backpack sat nearby, still unzipped.

Suddenly, somewhere in the darkness, Pete coughed. He stumbled to his feet, looking back in confusion at the accident.

"Mama?" he called weakly.

There was no response. Pete's vision swam. It felt as if he had just stepped out of a dream, everything blurred. He looked down and saw the storybook at his feet.

Uncertain, Pete leaned down to pick up the book. He clutched it to his chest with one hand, picking up his backpack with the other.

Pete waited alone in the dark for a long time. Finally, not knowing what else to do, the young boy sat down and started to put the book back into his backpack, pulling at the zipper. It still wouldn't close. Tears began to trickle down Pete's cheeks. He knew something bad had happened, and he felt scared and alone.

Suddenly, a loud howl echoed through the forest.

Pete jumped and clutched the storybook even more tightly. He peered into the trees, toward where the sound had come from. A pair of gleaming eyes peered back at him. Then another pair. And another. By the light of the stars Pete could make out the shapes of the creatures that were staring at him. Wolves.

Heavy growls escaped from behind their bared fangs. Pete turned and blindly ran away from the wild animals.

As he crashed through the trees, the forest grew thicker. A wolf howled. It sounded close, but when Pete looked back, all he could see were trees. Then came another howl, this time from somewhere up ahead. Pete whipped to face forward too late, and he stumbled over a branch, dropping his book as he crashed headlong into the uneven ground.

Sore and bruised, Pete got to his feet. The wolves were surrounding him, forming a tight circle. Pete's heart pounded so loudly he was sure the wolves could hear it.

There was nowhere to run. No one to run to.

BOOM.

Suddenly, a deep sound resonated throughout the forest like thunder. The trees shook.

BOOM.

And again. The wolves hesitated. They sniffed the air, growling at the sky.

BOOM.

Even louder. Pete looked around. He had no idea what was happening. A heavy wind pushed the tree branches back and forth. The cold Pacific air felt electric.

BOOM.

The wolves had had enough. They yelped in fright and scampered away. The treetops were moving more violently now, swaying and shaking as if something large . . . something *huge* was approaching.

Pete knew he should run, but his feet wouldn't move. He could barely breathe.

Brave, the boy thought. *I have to be brave!*

The trees swayed open like a gate, and a monstrous figure stepped out from among the towering pines. It was bigger than any animal Pete had ever seen. Bigger than anything Pete had ever imagined.

The ground shook with each step of the tremendous beast. A sliver of moonlight shone through the fog, and suddenly Pete could see the creature's face clearly.

He gasped.

It was a DRAGON! Green and surprisingly furry, with four huge feet the size of large tires, massive wings that arched up to the sky, and a long pointed tail like a dinosaur's.

Now, Pete had no way of knowing it was a dragon. He had never read about dragons in any of his storybooks. All he knew was that the creature was huge . . . and probably hungry.

The dragon turned its head back and forth. Pete could see its bright glowing eyes scanning the forest.

The young boy held his breath. Maybe the creature wouldn't notice him. Unfortunately, the cold air had turned bitter. Pete sniffled.

The tiny sound startled the large dragon. It jumped back, its fur rippling and standing on end. It whipped its head back and forth rapidly, searching for the source of the noise.

Finally, its gaze landed on the lonely little boy with tears running down his face.

The dragon studied Pete for a long moment. Then, slowly, it padded up to him.

Pete shuffled uncertainly, his eyes wide.

"Are you gonna eat me?" he asked.

The dragon leaned in, craning its long neck down toward Pete until they were face to face. It blinked curiously, like a puppy might look at a stranger. A deep sound rumbled in the massive creature's chest. But it didn't sound threatening. Instead it almost seemed warm and friendly. Like a deep purr.

Pete couldn't help smiling a little. He reached up and wiped the tears from his cheeks with the back of his hand.

Noticing the backpack on the ground, the dragon nudged it toward the boy with its snout. To Pete, it almost seemed like the creature wanted him to pick it up. So he bent down and grasped it. When he looked back up, he saw the beast extending its massive paw to him, like an invitation.

Pete wasn't sure what to do. The creature seemed friendly. And it had scared away the wolves. But could he trust it?

The dragon extended its paw farther. It made the purring sound again, and Pete looked deep into the creature's glowing eyes. He couldn't explain it, but the creature's expression seemed caring. He could tell it wanted to help him.

Pete took one last look in the direction of the accident and then turned away, climbing into the padding of the dragon's paw. So soft and comforting . . . Pete couldn't help curling up there.

The dragon lifted Pete and held him close enough that the boy could hear the great beast's heart beating deep in its chest. The dragon's fur rippled, shifting in color to match the colors of Pete's clothing.

The forest's silence was broken by the heavy sound of large wings beating against the wind. Swiftly, the pair rose into the dark night sky, flying high above the treetops.

Pete gasped. Flying. He was flying!

And in that moment, curled up in the safe warmth of the dragon's paw, everything that had happened to Pete became too much. Too much to process, too much to handle. And Pete felt very sleepy.

He nestled deeper into the dragon's fur and closed his eyes. Against the sound of the rushing wind and deep, rhythmic beating of the dragon's wings, Pete fell asleep.

CHAPTER THREE

"All my life, I've heard about the dragons that live in the woods."

The voice belonged to Mr. Conrad Meacham, an older man with thinning light hair and heavy smile lines at the corners of his mouth. Everyone knew Mr. Meacham. He had lived in the sleepy logging town of Millhaven all his life and could typically be found in his workshop with the large garage door swung open, entertaining the neighborhood children with his stories.

Mr. Meacham pushed a hand-carved piece of wood into place on a chair as he spoke. All around his workshop were bits and pieces of handmade furniture in various states of completion—most of them carved or fashioned with a dragon motif of some kind.

"Since the first man came here and chopped down a tree, the same stories have been told," Mr. Meacham was saying. "People say they came from the north. They say they're thousands of years old. They say there used to be many, but now there are few."

A group of anxious children sat on the garage floor, surrounding the old furniture maker. There was close to a dozen of them, and they were completely engrossed in Mr. Meacham's story. The kids had heard the old man's tales before, of course—some many times—but that never seemed to stop them from coming back for more.

Mr. Meacham waved away the sawdust drifting through the air. It billowed in the sunlight, sparkling throughout the garage like little flakes of gold dust.

"They say a lot of things, but so far as I know, not one person has ever actually seen a dragon. . . ." Mr. Meacham lowered himself onto a stool and leaned in closer to his captivated audience. "Except for me."

"*You* saw a dragon?" One little boy stared up in shock. Younger than most of the other children, he was newer to the stories than they were.

"Yes, sir," Mr. Meacham replied. "When I was a little boy—not much older than you—I was out hunting with my father, deep in those woods.

I wandered off on my own . . . and that's when I saw it."

"What'd it look like?" the little boy pressed.

Mr. Meacham chuckled. "Well, it was big, I can tell you that much. Big as a barn. And when it moved, the whole earth would shake." Mr. Meacham narrowed his eyes and focused in on the little boy. "It was green—green all over—except its eyes. Its eyes were red as hellfire. When it looked at me, it was peering into my very soul."

"And then . . . ?" The young children were on the edges of their seats.

"And then it roared!" Mr. Meacham exclaimed. "I thought I was done for. And sure enough, before I could even blink, it reared back with its terrible claws and . . ."

The old man swiped his hand in the air for emphasis, causing the startled children to jump backward.

"I never had a chance. I fell to the ground, and it was on top of me. Everything happened so fast. I could feel its jaws closing on my arm. I could feel those teeth sinking in!"

A glint came to Mr. Meacham's eye. "But I wasn't ready. No, sir. It wasn't my time just yet. With my free hand I grabbed this pocketknife. . . ."

Mr. Meacham jumped up and seized a

pocketknife from his garage workbench. Old and dull and stained with red rust, the blade still looked sharp enough to the children. He flashed the knife back and forth, reenacting his battle with the dragon.

"And I drove the blade home."

With that, Mr. Meacham slammed the tip of the knife into the surface of the workbench. It struck with a loud, dull thunk.

"I got it," Mr. Meacham continued. "I got it good. The dragon roared to high heaven and I could see blood where I'd struck it. I didn't waste my breath—I rolled out of the way, scrambled to my feet, and stood up, ready to fight . . . only to find the dragon . . ."

The children held their breath.

". . . had disappeared," Mr. Meacham finished dramatically. "Vanished without a trace."

"But . . . why?" asked the little boy.

Mr. Meacham shrugged and unbuttoned the cuff of his flannel sleeve. "Who knows? Maybe I scared it off. The only evidence that it had ever been there at all is right here. . . ."

He rolled up his shirtsleeve and the children gasped. All along Mr. Meacham's left arm were deep, jagged scars that looked quite a bit like bite marks.

"Scaring the neighborhood kids again, Dad?"

Everyone's eyes turned toward the voice. Standing just outside the workshop doors was Grace Meacham, Mr. Meacham's daughter. She was a pretty young woman dressed in a green forest ranger uniform, with long red hair tied back in a braid. Her amused smile and gentle eye roll gave a good indication of just how many times she had heard her dad tell that story before.

"Aw, they're not scared. I'm giving them a leg up," her father replied. "They need to know what's out there in this big world around them. . . ."

Grace shook her head, laughing tiredly. She and her father had debated this argument more times than she could remember.

"Well, I'm out in the woods every day," she said. "I've seen bears, bobcats, badgers, bunnies, and just about every type of bird you could imagine . . . but no dragons."

"Those woods go on for hundreds of miles." Mr. Meacham waved his hand. "I reckon there might be a few nooks and crannies you've overlooked."

Grace held up her binoculars as she walked to her jeep. "I wouldn't count on that—but I'll be sure to give you a call if I see anything big and green that can breathe fire. . . ."

She climbed into the car and started the engine.

Meanwhile, the littlest girl in the crowd turned back to Mr. Meacham, her eyes wide with wonder.

"It can breathe fire?"

Mr. Meacham returned his attention to the young audience in front of him.

"Well, I was getting to that part. Don't go listening to Grace. She knows a thing or two, but only if it's staring her in the face."

The hum of Grace's jeep faded away as it drove off toward the forest. Mr. Meacham plucked his old knife out of the workbench and picked up a small, simple wooden dragon. It was one of the very first things he had ever carved.

"If you go through the world only looking at what's right in front of you, you miss out on a whole lot. And that's where you have the upper hand. Because mark my words . . ."

Mr. Meacham handed the little girl the delicate wooden dragon. All the kids gathered around her to look at it.

"That dragon is still out there," Mr. Meacham whispered. "And if you were to go out into those woods, where no one ever goes, maybe . . . maybe one of *you* might find it."

With a small laugh and a wink he snatched the wooden dragon back from the enthralled children.

"Unless it finds you first."

CHAPTER FOUR

The forest was still and quiet.

Out from the deep brush, a small and very furry rabbit appeared. The rabbit sniffed the air tentatively, as it was young and inexperienced in the ways of the wilderness. Still, it knew to be careful of predators. The rabbit hopped cautiously toward the nearby gully—a good place to find water.

A brook babbled up ahead. The rabbit hopped more quickly. But as it reached the edge of the brook, it stopped. It sniffed.

Suddenly, a boy jumped out from the underbrush and grabbed the bunny with two hands, scooping it up in a rolling tumble.

The boy laughed in delight. *He* was certainly

not new to the forest, and he loved playing games with the small creatures that lived there. But the boy had not lived his whole life in the woods. In fact, he didn't really belong there at all.

The boy was none other than Pete.

It had been several years since the night of the car crash. Pete looked taller than before, leaner, with much of his baby fat burned away by time. And his skin was darkened from years playing in the sun. The clothes he had been wearing when he'd arrived in the forest had been reduced to tatters. What used to be corduroy pants were now threadbare shorts. His shirt was gone altogether. And Pete's hair had grown out into ratty tangles.

Pete rolled upright, holding the rabbit and smiling. Somehow, the rabbit knew Pete wasn't dangerous. It didn't bite or fight back. Instead, it simply wriggled its nose. Pete wriggled his nose in response and gently placed the rabbit back on the ground.

Suddenly, both Pete and the rabbit stopped. A new smell had entered the scene—one far less friendly. . . .

A huge brown bear had spotted them from the creek bed a few feet away.

Not hesitating a beat, the rabbit vanished into the deep underbrush.

Left alone, Pete stared at the bear.

"Bear-er-er . . ." he whispered under his breath. The bear responded by rising onto its hind legs, fur bristling around its neck. It let out an angry bellow—a powerful rumble that could be heard all across the forest.

Pete grinned, unfazed by the display. He clenched his fists tightly together, squared his shoulders, and took a massive breath. Then he let out the loudest and most powerful cry he could. It went on and on, echoing farther and louder than even the bear's roar. For an eleven-year-old boy, it was quite impressive!

But perhaps not impressive enough to scare off a large grizzly bear.

The bear padded forward, moving closer and closer to the boy. It looked like Pete was about to become the bear's lunch!

And then, without warning, it stopped. The bear stood completely still. It turned and ran! Pete watched it scamper away. His cry must have frightened it after all.

Pete grinned from ear to ear, the feeling of triumph warming him in the cool northwest air.

Suddenly, he heard a rustle behind him and looked around to see a dragon emerging from the woods. His dragon. Pete's grin grew wider. He hadn't scared the bear away. His dragon had! Pete threw his arms open in greeting, yelling out the only name he could have ever given to the giant furry friend who had saved him from that cold, dark night so very long before.

"Elliot!"

The pair bounded into the creek, heading toward their daily adventures.

CHAPTER FIVE

For Pete and his dragon, it was a day like every other day. Pete carefully moved through the thickets of blackberries along a steep and rocky slope. After years of practice, the boy knew exactly where to find the juiciest fruits in the forest. One by one he plucked the berries and popped them into his mouth.

Nearby, a loud crash echoed through the woods as Elliot tried his own fruit-picking method—grabbing a large bush with his powerful jaws and shaking it back and forth. Pete laughed with his arms spread out, catching as much of the raining fruit as he could. Then, with a single gulp, the dragon swallowed the rest of the blackberry bush—vines and thorns and all.

Once they were through with their afternoon snack, the friends rushed down the gully and into the cold, clean river that cut through the woods. Pete splashed at the water, making his reflection ripple and swirl. Elliot wanted to make his reflection ripple, too. The dragon did a huge belly flop into the deepest part of the river. It made an enormous wave that washed up and over Pete! The boy splashed back to the surface, laughing. Elliot was always doing silly things like that.

Full and happy, Pete took off running up a steep hill lined with tall pine trees. The large trunk of an older tree had fallen at an angle, forming a natural ramp up to the treetops. Pete scampered up the old trunk, gaining speed with every step. Within moments he was high among the branches, running quickly and confidently enough that there was no chance he would lose his balance; this was a path he knew very well.

Reaching the trunk's end, Pete leaped straight off and out into the air. There was nothing between him and the ground, save a hundred feet or so. And suddenly, there was Elliot, perfectly positioned for Pete to land on his back. The dragon caught Pete! With a whoop, Pete slid feetfirst down the dragon's tail and landed safely on the ground.

Pete whirled immediately back toward Elliot.

But the dragon had disappeared without a trace. . . .

"Elliot?" Pete asked the empty air, knowing what the response would be.

Pete made an exaggerated show of looking to his left. As he did, a sneaky green tail slithered down from above, carefully and quickly tapping the young boy on the right shoulder.

Pete instinctively jumped. He looked up, trying to catch the dragon in the act—but he was already too late. For the quickest of moments, Elliot's head appeared behind the boy. The dragon nudged the back of Pete's neck with his long nose, then retreated backward.

Pete whirled again—and again it was too late. Where Elliot had been only a second before, there were just trees.

Suddenly, the forest shifted and wavered, like a mirage on a hot day. Elliot was right there, in plain sight, yet completely and thoroughly camouflaged. Pete had learned long ago that Elliot was able to change his color to blend in with his surroundings, sometimes even vanishing altogether as though he wasn't there. The dragon returned to his normal green color and happily rolled over on his back, pleased with his game of hide-and-seek.

With a laugh, Pete returned to the business of running, racing toward a nearby cliff edge. The trees thinned out rapidly, revealing nothing but the bluest of skies for miles and miles. The soft ground under Pete's feet soon gave way to hard rock. Up ahead, the dizzying drop to the wooded valley below grew closer and closer, but Pete didn't slow his pace. He simply ran as far as the terrain would allow and, with a massive leap, disappeared over the edge of the cliff.

Less than a moment later, the dragon swooped down after him. Then Elliot rocketed skyward, with Pete on his back. The boy gripped Elliot's thick fur in both hands, shouting loudly in exhilaration as the dragon soared through the sky. They flew up and down as though they were on a roller coaster, skimming treetops and banking in midair to fly back up toward the sun.

Fearless, Pete let go with both hands and threw his head back, laughing all the way. They broke through the clouds and flew far above the world, where they could see everything—the clumps of treetops, the green meadows, the rushing river that looked no bigger than a creek. With one last quick twist, Elliot turned downward, plunging toward the earth.

Down they spiraled, the surface of the world rising quickly to greet them. Just before the great green dragon would have slammed into the ground, he pulled up sharply, angling his large body so they were gliding above the river. It was so close that Elliot's massive paws skimmed the cold surface, sending a long spray of water to either side as they went.

The dragon and the boy plunged into the deepest and darkest part of the massive northwestern forest. The small amount of daylight that managed to pierce the thick canopy of trees cut through the long shadows in wide beams, adding just enough light to see. Pete and Elliot moved quickly over a large ridge thick with towering pines and then down toward one tree in particular.

It was tremendous—unlike any other tree in the forest, as ancient as it was towering. At its base, knobby roots encircled a dragon-sized cave that ran deep into the earth. And above, built into the tree's gnarled limbs, was a tree house—exactly the type of tree house a wild eleven-year-old might build. It was ingenious and scrappy-looking, everything bound together with vines and mud. There were different levels and gnarled branch walkways and wooden ladders and vine ropes. It all culminated in a thatched crow's nest above the uppermost branches.

This was their home.

Pete scrambled up the trunk using handholds

and footholds gouged into the bark. He made it to the first platform and then crossed a makeshift bridge. Soon he was at the very top. Pete threw his head back and let out a howl. Elliot, at the base of the tree, pointed his large head to the sky and howled along. Their voices—both high and low, soft and loud—echoed far into the distance.

If anyone could have seen Pete in that very moment—anyone who had known him in the time before the crash—they would never have recognized him.

Pete himself could barely remember that other life. He only knew the forest. And the wind. And the bright blue sky that he and Elliot soared through each day.

And Elliot. Pete knew Elliot was his family. Of that he was certain.

CHAPTER SIX

One day, something different happened.

Pete and Elliot had a plan to spend the morning exploring. There was always something new to do in the forest—a new rock to pry up and look under, or a new tree to climb. And so they wandered among the incredibly tall pine trees until soon they were somewhere they had never been before.

Pete turned to Elliot, about to ask which way they should go. Suddenly, he heard footsteps. They were light and quiet, but to Pete they may as well have been as loud as thunder. Pete knew every sound every animal in the forest might make, and this one was different.

Elliot instinctively vanished, and Pete ducked

behind a fallen tree. A moment later, the boy's curiosity got the better of him. Pete lifted his head to take a peek, suddenly seeing . . .

He wasn't sure at first. A . . . person? Walking through the forest? The boy's jaw dropped. It was a woman! He hadn't seen anyone but Elliot and the other forest animals for a long, long time.

"There you are." The woman spoke. Pete froze. He was hiding perfectly. How could she see him? Why did she seem to know him already?

With a quick upward glance, Pete realized that he wasn't actually the one the woman was speaking to. She was speaking to a bird, a spotted owl, in the lower branches of a nearby tree. The tree had a strange red marking on it—something Pete hadn't noticed before.

Somewhere in the back of his mind, Pete could sense Elliot's nervousness. The large dragon had faded to match the colors and patterns of the surrounding trees so perfectly that he might as well have been invisible.

Pete watched as the woman brushed back a stray strand of hair from her face. Instinctively, he reached up and mimicked the motion, brushing his own hair away from his eyes.

A woman in the forest.

What could it mean?

* * *

Grace brushed the hair out of her eyes and shook her head. The marking she had found—the red X—was far from where it should have been.

Grace pulled her compass out of her satchel. She remembered when her father had first given it to her so many years before. It had seemed like a magical artifact—one that opened to reveal a delicate star design and an arrow that swung around until it found north. It was old even when she was a child but very well taken care of. Grace had always been able to find her way with it.

She opened it and sighed. The loggers were moving far beyond the territories allotted to them, marking and chopping down trees they weren't supposed to. With a swift movement, she returned the compass to her satchel and placed the bag on the stump of a recently cut tree. Just as quickly, she removed another item—a can of blue spray paint. Grace painted a blue flourish over the red on the tree with the owl in it.

"No one's gonna cut you down now," she said.

Just then, she was interrupted by the sound of a branch snapping. Grace whirled, startled.

"Ready to go, Grace?"

That voice belonged to another ranger, John

Wentworth. Grace had worked with him for the past few years. He was a man of few words. But Wentworth was excellent at his job, and Grace appreciated his help in the forest.

"Yeah . . ." Grace replied. She reached for her satchel and picked it up from the stump. Giving one last look around, she followed her coworker back to the loggers' job site.

Grace's jeep was parked in the middle of the newly open expanse. Sitting next to it was a backhoe: a large, bright yellow piece of digging machinery.

Grace's boot bumped into something. She glanced down to see a glass bottle with a smiley-face logo, now empty. Litter left over from the loggers. Grace picked it up and sighed. She looked at the backhoe, and a purposeful glint formed in her eyes.

"Just one second," she said to Ranger Wentworth as she approached the backhoe. After climbing inside, she reached up to the vehicle's sun visor. Sure enough, Grace's search was rewarded with a set of jingly keys. *Bingo*. She held them up to show Wentworth. Then she promptly tossed the keys into the dirt several feet away.

Ranger Wentworth let out an audible sigh. "Oh, come on, Grace. Not again . . ."

Grace shrugged. "I'm just settling a score."

"One for Jack, one for you, huh?" Wentworth asked.

"Something like that," Grace replied vaguely.

Their task in that part of the forest complete, the two rangers jumped into the jeep and headed off. As Grace drove down the bumpy logging road, she saw more and more trees marked with the tell-tale red paint.

It was going to be a long day.

* * *

Pete had been immediately drawn to the strange woman, especially after she'd held up the shiny disk from her bag. Bit by bit, the young boy had snuck silently up behind her. And while the woman had painted a blue marking on the tree, he had carefully removed the glimmering treasure from her satchel.

Then the woman had been met by another person—a man—and they'd headed off together. Pete watched, fascinated, as they left. They were people. In the forest. Who knew what other treasures they had?

Pete followed the people.

He looked around in wonder as they passed more and more trees with the strange blue mark.

It was almost as though they were tracing a specific path through the forest. Taking it all in, Pete momentarily lost sight of the two strangers. He shook his head and continued following the trail of the blue-marked trees, determined not to lose them.

Suddenly, there was no more forest.

Where there had once been trees remained nothing but dirt: acres of cleared land dotted with a few leftover stumps.

"The trees ran away," Pete whispered.

He stood frozen in surprise at the edge of the clearing, watching the man and the woman get into a vehicle and drive away.

Pete walked into the empty space, trying to figure out just what that part of the forest *was*. Why it was so different from the rest.

Elliot appeared behind Pete. The dragon sniffed the air, and his face sagged with sadness as he looked over the empty patch of forest. *So many lost friends*, his eyes seemed to say. Then the dragon stepped backward, bumping into a big yellow vehicle. With a casual push, he knocked the massive piece of digging equipment onto its side.

Just then, a metallic glint caught Pete's eye. He ran ahead to pick up the discarded ring of keys. Aha! At least there was more treasure! With a gleeful smile, the boy pulled the silver disk from his pocket and compared the two shiny bits of metal. The disk was infinitely more fascinating than the keys, and Pete lingered over it. It was shiny . . . so shiny it almost caused Pete's face to glow.

Elliot bent down and sniffed the antique, then let out a massive dragon sneeze. The force of it knocked Pete off his feet.

"Ewww!" Pete said, shaking off dragon-sneeze goop. Then the boy realized he had dropped the shiny thing. When he bent down to pick it up, the disk was *open*. Pete hadn't known it *could* open. He stared at it, captivated.

Painted inside the disk were drawings. Pete reached into the back of his brain to remember what they were called—*letters*. N, S, W, and E, surrounding what looked like a large star. An arrow rested on top of the star, shifting slightly as Pete tilted the disk. Then he saw a picture taped inside the lid: a faded snapshot of three people. A little girl. A man. And a woman . . .

Pete sat down, overcome by a rush of feelings he hadn't felt in a very long time.

A picture of a father . . . a daughter . . . and a mother.

A *family*.

CHAPTER SEVEN

It was a late night for Pete. Not that he minded. He had already been on an adventure that day. Now he was doing his second favorite thing after exploring the forest—building traps.

Pete gathered several of the toughest vines he could find near the tree house. He carefully wove the ends together while Elliot moved some large logs to the places Pete had marked. Eventually, after tying together several of the vines and running them around a handful of trees, Pete knew his trap was ready.

It wasn't that Pete expected unwanted visitors. But he had been creating traps since he first started living in the forest. Simple ones in the beginning—trip wires, holes covered with pine branches, that sort of thing. But after years and years of practice, his trap-making skills had become pretty impressive. And he really liked inventing new ones.

In between moving logs, Elliot was doing *his* second-favorite activity: hunting his own wiggling tail. Elliot was obsessed with trying to catch his tail. And though the great green dragon was sly and crafty, every time he pounced, his tail managed to zip away just before he could catch it. This night was no different.

Elliot jumped to the left. A near miss! He jumped again. His tail flicked just out of reach. Oh, so close! The dragon leaped a third time. . . .

Pete looked up. Elliot was jumping right next to the trap he had just rigged. The dragon was about to spring it!

"Look out!" Pete cried. But it was too late. With one big pounce, Elliot leaped directly through the trip wire. Down came the log, swinging perfectly from its suspension point in the canopy of the forest. The dragon dove out of the way in the nick of time, turning back to growl at the log like an angry dog.

Pete laughed so hard he clutched his stomach. Well, at least they knew the trap worked.

Just then, the sky started to rumble and darken. The telltale smell of rain wafted through the forest.

With a quick and concentrated effort, Pete and Elliot reset the trap and then took refuge in Elliot's cave underneath.

Pete grabbed a few sticks and some kindling. He started setting up a warm campfire in the center of the cavern. As the rain started to pitter-patter outside, Elliot pawed at the dirt floor, turning around a few times before finding the perfect spot to settle.

Pete sat down also and snuggled against Elliot's warm fur. The fire glowed brightly, giving off a comforting heat throughout the entire cavern. It was so nice and cozy. This was always one of Pete's favorite times of day. Just him and Elliot, safe and happy and together.

Pete picked up a familiar storybook from the ground nearby—the same book he had been reading the night he arrived in the forest. He flipped through the pages of the tattered, berry-juice-stained book. Then he picked up a slightly burned stick and started to draw on one of the pages. The ashes marked the paper with dense, chalky lines. The entire book was covered in similar markings—made with ash and mud and juice.

Elliot shifted, looking curiously over Pete's shoulder as the boy worked. Pete pointed to an image in the book—a picture of a car.

"Pete. Elliot. Vrooooom . . ." he said.

Pete turned the book upside down. "And then everything's . . ." He flipped the book over and over, mimicking the way his family's car had flipped in the accident. He had told this story to Elliot many times before, and he knew the motions by heart.

"And Pete and Elliot go down and down . . ."

Pete dropped the book. It's impact on the ground caused Elliot to flinch.

". . . and then they're all alone," Pete finished.

Elliot moaned in response. He hated that part of the story. Pete patted him reassuringly.

"Don't worry," he said. "Someday I'll be big like you and we'll find our own family."

Elliot nudged Pete and made the soft purring noise deep in his chest. That meant he agreed. Pete looked at the page the book had landed on, an image of a little lost puppy at night, under a moon and three yellow stars. The picture was missing something, Pete felt.

With his burnt stick in hand, Pete scraped lines and letters around the biggest star: *N, S, W, E.* The simple star on the page had been transformed into the inside of the magical disk. Almost without thinking, Pete slipped his hand into his pocket and took out the treasure he had stolen. Even as he spun it around in his hand, the little red needle continued to point in only one direction.

Pete looked in that direction—north. "I wonder where that lady came from," he whispered. Elliot responded with only a soft growl.

Yawning, Pete snuggled in. "Don't worry. I won't let her hurt you."

Elliot yawned back. Nestled together safe and sound by the glowing fire, the boy and the dragon were soon fast asleep.

CHAPTER EIGHT

Whirrrrrrrr.

It was a bright and shining morning. The birds were chirping. Sunlight streamed into Pete and Elliot's cave. But there was a strange noise outside. A different noise. One that definitely didn't belong in the forest.

Whirrrrrrrrrrrrrr.

Pete jerked awake. He tapped Elliot's arm, but the dragon barely opened one eye. Instead, Elliot shifted and went back to sleep.

The strange mechanical noise filled the cave again. The chirping birds took off loudly, angry at the disturbance.

Pete glanced back at the snoring dragon. He knew from experience that it was impossible to wake Elliot up if he didn't want to be woken. So Pete scampered outside alone, curious to see what was causing such a commotion. Outside the safety and warmth of the cave, Pete scurried across the forest, closer and closer to the strange sounds. As he did so, new noises drifted to his ears. The whining buzz of a chainsaw. A man yelling, "Timberrr!" And a sharp cracking that rang through the entire forest.

Pete reached the top of a hill, taking in the sight of the source of all that noise. And what he saw made him gasp.

Down at the bottom of the hill were more yellow vehicles—big flatbeds rolling through the forest. And men—a crew of loggers, ten or so total—all wearing identical orange hard hats. It was more people than Pete could remember ever seeing at one time, and the boy felt a strange combination of nervousness and excitement. And fear. He didn't know what exactly the machines were. But he could tell that they were cutting down trees and hauling them away. And that made Pete feel afraid.

But before he could respond to any of those warring emotions, something else caught his eye: the trees had all been marked with red paint, angry slashes down the side of each trunk.

* * *

Gavin Magary stood on the stump of a fallen tree. He smoothed his jet-black hair and took a swig of his ginger ale. A hunting rifle was slung over his shoulder. It shifted, glinting in the sunlight. Just as Gavin was about to adjust it, he snapped to attention. There was a faint rustle in the distance. Squinting, he searched the trees until he found it—a deer grazing many yards away.

Gavin carefully set down his soda and slid the hunting rifle off his shoulder. Bringing the scope up to his eye, he focused on the animal. Of course, the deer wasn't dangerous. But Gavin was a hunter, and he had a perfect shot. He focused his gaze, tensed his trigger finger, and—

"This is out of line, Jack!"

Gavin turned toward the sound, letting out a long, exasperated sigh. Unsurprisingly, the voice belonged to Grace, the park ranger and girlfriend of his brother, Jack, who was in fact marching right alongside her.

Grace continued yelling. "Gavin *knows* he's not supposed to be cutting this deep! How'd he even cut this road out here?"

Jack gently pulled Grace aside, attempting to turn the conversation in a more calm direction. "Grace . . . please . . . let me handle this—"

"You *don't* handle it," Grace interrupted. "That's

the problem! If I don't do anything there won't be any forest left for either of us!"

"I know, I know . . . he made a mistake—"

"What's that?" Gavin shouted toward the couple. If they were talking about him, he might as well get a word in.

Jack just kept talking, ignoring his brother. "But all I'm asking is that you take two steps to the left and look at things from my perspective here."

"I bend over backward to see things from your perspective every single day!" Grace retorted. "Why won't you ever take a stand for what I care about? I thought we were in this together!"

Gavin clicked his tongue. It looked like everything was business as usual. He turned his attention from the bickering couple back to the tree line. The deer was gone. Figured.

* * *

Meanwhile, Pete was still watching from the top of the hill. He listened to the adults arguing. But their voices were muffled by distance, and he couldn't really hear what they were saying. A moment later, his attention drifted to a nearby truck.

The passenger door opened abruptly, catching Pete by surprise. There was another person inside, a young girl about Pete's age.

"Hey!" the girl called out to the man arguing with the woman. "I have to get to school!"

Looking over his shoulder, the man yelled back to the little girl. "Just give me one more minute, sweetheart. . . ."

Pete was now thoroughly enthralled. It was so interesting the way those people interacted with each other, so different from the way the animals communicated.

Down below, the little girl kicked at the dirt with her toe. Pete watched as she started to wander around the open logging area, meandering from stump to stump. Suddenly, she spotted a red bird overhead on a tree branch. She followed it with her eyes as it darted up and flew deeper into the forest. Pete was watching the girl intently . . . when he realized she was staring directly at him.

A startled expression crossed the girl's face.

Pete had been spotted!

He quickly turned and dashed back into the woods.

"Hey, wait! Don't go!" she yelled after him.

CHAPTER NINE

Natalie Magary didn't wait for any of the adults to take notice. Instead she ran after the strange-looking boy as fast as she could.

The voices of the grown-ups grew more and more distant. The boy was just ahead of Natalie. She had a feeling he was purposely running slow so she could keep up with him.

"What are you doing out here?" she yelled after him. "Are you lost?"

The boy didn't respond. Instead, he showed off a bit by jumping over logs and swinging from low branches on his way through the ever thickening woods. Natalie tried hard to follow the boy's movements and did an okay job of it . . . mostly.

Then he was gone. Natalie whirled around, not sure how she had lost track of the boy.

"Hello . . . ?" she called out hesitantly.

A sudden snap above her caused her to jump. The forest boy was climbing into the trees, practically camouflaged by the leaves and branches.

"How'd you get up there?" she asked. There was no response.

Natalie grabbed the lowest branch and started to haul herself up, too. Pete stopped, looking down at her curiously. But as soon as their eyes made contact, he climbed even higher before resting on a sturdy branch.

Slowly, Natalie reached the branch where the boy was perched. She clung tightly to the trunk of the tree. It wasn't really that high up, but still . . . it was high enough. The boy, on the other hand, kicked his legs casually, seemingly unconcerned and unafraid.

"What's your name?" Natalie asked, out of breath.

Instead of answering, the boy jumped upward, grabbing another branch. With one quick and practiced motion, he pulled himself up even higher.

Natalie groaned. "Oh, come on. Slow down!"

Despite the irritation in her voice, Natalie was excited—so she kept climbing.

The pair continued the chase, farther and farther up the tree. Natalie's palms grew clammy. They were up very high now. But she wasn't going to let that stop her.

"You're pretty good at this," Natalie managed between breaths. "Do your parents know you're out here?"

The boy tilted his head, appearing confused by the question.

"Are you all alone?" Natalie continued.

That one seemed easier to answer. He shook his head vehemently.

"Elliot."

"Elliot?" Natalie frowned, confused.

"Elliot," Pete repeated.

Natalie took a deep breath, still clinging tightly to the tree.

"Where's Elliot?" she asked.

The boy responded by pointing out in the distance.

Suddenly, a gust of wind blew, rustling Natalie's clothes and hair. Unfortunately, she made the mistake of looking down. . . .

"Whoa," Natalie said.

Her heart began to race. "I should probably get down. . . ."

With a careful step, Natalie attempted to reverse the climb that had taken her so high. But the combination of nerves and fear and the loss of the adrenaline she had felt while chasing the young boy all made the return trip far more difficult.

She immediately began to slip, both feet skidding down the tree trunk. Then she was dangling, holding on to a branch with one hand. One of her shoes slipped off and fell for a terrifying amount of time before reaching the ground.

And then, with a scream, she lost her grip entirely.

CHAPTER TEN

Pete acted on instinct, lunging forward and grabbing Natalie by the arm. It was a precarious position for both of them. Pete was awkwardly balanced, holding on to Natalie. And he saw that Natalie's feet couldn't quite reach a tree limb. . . .

Mustering all his strength, Pete planted his own feet on the branch below for leverage as he hauled the young girl upward. It would have worked if the branch had been just a little bit stronger.

With a sharp snap the branch broke, and both Pete and Natalie lost all support. They plummeted, Natalie screaming all the way, until—

Pete miraculously landed feetfirst on a sturdy bough! He grabbed hold of Natalie's arm as she sped past him. She jerked to a stop, her weight pulling at Pete. But the young boy managed to keep his footing on the branch.

Now Natalie was dangling from Pete's hand as he gripped a branch above for balance. "Don't let go!" she yelled, afraid to look down.

Pete tried, but his hand was slippery and Natalie was just too heavy. She slid out of his grip.

"No!" Natalie screamed as she fell again.

* * *

Thunk! Natalie's cry had barely escaped her lips before she landed with a soft thud. As it turned out, the ground had been only a few feet below. She hadn't realized how close she was to landing when Pete caught her. She was safe.

Natalie sat upright in a daze, patting at herself to make 100 percent sure she was still alive.

The strange forest boy dropped down from the branch he had been standing on, shrugging silently as he did so. Then he caught sight of Natalie's knee; it had been scraped in the fall. He reached out to touch it, but Natalie flinched.

"Don't!" Natalie said. "I'm hurt. . . ."

The boy looked at her curiously and instead used his outstretched hand to wipe a tiny tear from the corner of Natalie's eye. She hadn't even realized she was crying.

"How old are you?" she asked.

The boy thought hard for a moment. It didn't seem like he knew the answer.

"Ffffive . . . ?" he replied with an uncertain shrug.

Natalie raised an eyebrow. "You're pretty big for a five-year-old."

The boy shrugged again. Natalie decided to try a different angle. "You never told me your name."

This time the boy answered quickly and confidently. "Pete!" he said, pointing his thumb at himself.

"You look like a Pete," Natalie said. "My name's—"

"Natalie!" someone cried from not far away. It was Natalie's father, Jack. He was rushing toward them in a panic. Grace and the rest of the logging crew followed him.

"Natalie!" Jack said. "My god—you can't run off like that! You could get hurt or—" He looked at her dirty hands and ripped jeans. "What happened to you?"

"I fell out of a tree," Natalie replied calmly.

Alarm crossed Jack's face. "What were you doing in a tree?"

"Following *him*." Natalie pointed behind her.

Jack stopped short. He and the rest of the adults turned, noticing Pete for the first time. As soon as the people had crashed through the trees, Pete had moved to the edge of the small clearing. Now the workers all stared at him in surprise. His tattered clothes and matted hair indicated he had been lost in the forest for a very long time.

"Pete," Natalie whispered. "His name is Pete."

"Pete?" Grace stepped forward. The boy backed away and hid behind a fallen trunk.

"Wait, wait," Grace said softly. "Hold on a second. . . ."

Pete didn't answer. It was clear he wanted to run. But he was also fascinated by Grace. Taking advantage of the boy's momentary hesitation, Grace stepped closer.

"Where did you come from? Where are your parents? Your family?"

Pete frowned. He didn't know what to say.

"I don't think he knows . . ." Natalie began.

Suddenly, as Pete shifted behind the tree, Grace noticed something glinting on the boy's neck.

"Hey," Grace said, recognizing her compass. "Where did you get that . . . ?"

That was enough for Pete. He turned and bolted—right into Gavin. The burly logger grabbed him by the shoulders.

"Whoa there, little buddy," said Gavin. "Where are you going so fast?"

"ELLIOT!" Pete yelled as loudly as he could.

Pete squirmed away, climbing up Gavin's large body and springing off him to a nearby tree.

"Don't hurt him!" Natalie yelled.

"I'm not gonna—" Gavin responded, reaching out quickly to grab at Pete's legs. "Come here, kid!"

Gavin tugged on Pete's ankle and pulled the young boy backward, harder than he intended.

Pete toppled, arms flailing. Unbalanced, he hit the ground headfirst.

For the second time in his life, everything went dark.

CHAPTER ELEVEN

Elliot stretched, waking up late in the morning. He had slept well. Very well.

And then the furry dragon realized that Pete was nowhere to be seen.

He checked the tree fort. No Pete.

He checked the river. No Pete.

He looked over at one of their favorite climbing stones. No Pete.

Where could he be?

Elliot pawed the ground, upset. Then he lifted his head and howled loudly, calling for his missing friend.

But there was no answer.

CHAPTER TWELVE

"Come on, Jack." Gavin's voice was tinged with frustration. "Give me a little credit at least."

The brothers were in the forest with only the other loggers for company, now that Grace and Natalie had taken Pete to the hospital. The loggers were packing up their trucks.

"I was just trying to take some initiative!" Gavin continued. "Help us compete with the big boys! You know how much these trees are worth?"

Jack sat on a nearby stump tiredly, looking around. There were a lot of newly cut trees now—a lot more than there should have been. He shook his head. "I'm not worried about the competition," he said. "I'm worried about my brother going behind my back. I'm worried about children getting hurt because we're not where we belong!"

Gavin rolled his eyes. "Aw, come on. If we hadn't been cutting out here, we wouldn't have found the kid in the first place. We're doing good work here, Jack!"

"And how about a few years from now, when we don't have anything left to cut down because you kept jumping the gun?" Jack countered. "What then? Grace just wants us to be responsible."

Gavin made a frustrated noise. "She wants to shut us down is what she wants!" Gavin said. "Don't tell me you're too whipped to see that!"

Jack frowned. "Help your men pack up. I want you and everyone else back on the eastern pad on Monday morning. I'll be back later."

"Where are you headed?" Gavin asked.

"Where do you think?" Jack snapped. "You're not the only family I've got to look after."

Gavin shuffled his feet. He didn't like being put in his place. Especially in front of the other loggers. "Yeah. Fine. Let me know how Natalie is doing. That Pete kid, too."

Jack nodded silently. He climbed into his truck and drove away.

One of the loggers, Woodrow, approached Gavin. "Jack giving you a hard time?"

Gavin waved away the question. "Jack's just

sore about his girlfriend stepping on his toes," he said. "He'll come around one of these days."

With a grunt, Gavin picked up a heavy generator and dropped it carelessly into the back of a truck. It made a loud clang.

Just then, not far away in the trees, there was another loud sound. *BOOM.*

Gavin looked up sharply. At the edge of the clearing, a large pine was falling down into the brush. But the loggers hadn't chopped that tree. Something big had knocked it over. Something *huge.*

Everyone stopped what they were doing.

"Huh," said a logger named Bobby.

"Looks like something's out there," Woodrow added.

"Something big," a third man named Abner said.

Gavin suddenly saw a chance to get rid of a little of the frustration he had been feeling. Picking up his rifle, he smiled as he glanced at the other loggers.

"Anyone feel like doing a little hunting?"

* * *

Normally, Elliot wouldn't have gone anywhere near the humans. But Pete was missing, and Elliot didn't know what else to do.

So he had edged up to the border of the forest—invisibly, of course—and listened.

It turned out that Elliot had wandered up in the middle of the argument between Gavin and Jack. He wasn't comfortable at all with being this close to the humans. But this was his best chance at finding his friend.

"Let me know how Natalie is doing. That Pete kid, too."

The dragon's ears perked up at the sound of Pete's name. So they *did* know where his friend was! Elliot thumped his tail in anticipation. He looked from human to human, wondering if one of them would lead him to Pete when they were done with whatever they were doing.

Just then, there was a loud clanging noise as Gavin threw the generator into the truck. The sound startled Elliot.

The dragon jumped backward . . . right into a tree. It fell with a thundering *BOOM*.

Elliot glanced back at the humans. They were pointing in his direction. They didn't look like they were going off to find Pete anytime soon. In fact, they looked like they were going to try to find *him*.

CHAPTER THIRTEEN

Pete couldn't see clearly. Everything was blurry. There was something floating above him . . . a tent? A tent billowing in the breeze? Pete couldn't place it. He was inside, and the walls were shifting. Was it a dream? Pete looked down at himself. He was five years old again.

Sunlight spilled into the tent, startling Pete. A face appeared. It was his mother. And she was smiling at him.

"Time to wake up, Pete," she said.

Suddenly, she was gone.

"Mama?"

Pete sat upright with a start. He was in a bed. In a hospital. He had been dreaming. The bright white light from his dream was an overhead fluorescent bulb. His eyes flitted around nervously. Everything in the room was white.

"Elliot . . . ?"

Pete glanced at the corner of the bed. There was a balloon tied there. He reached out and gently poked at the strange floating red circle. He'd seen one of those before, a long time ago.

The balloon drifted toward Pete. He hadn't been expecting that, and he jumped back abruptly.

Pete climbed off the bed, a little unsteady. He suddenly noticed a reflection in the hospital room window. Was that . . . him? Instead of the threadbare pants he had worn for the past several years, Pete was wearing clean pajamas. And his skin looked oddly pale and smooth with all the dirt washed away.

Pete didn't like it. It didn't look like him!

His thoughts were interrupted by voices. Carefully, he crept over to the other window in the room and peeked through the blinds. Unlike the window on the opposite wall, through which Pete could see outside, this window was strange. It opened up into a bright white hallway filled with activity and people Pete recognized from the forest.

People who were talking about him.

Pete didn't like this. He didn't want to be there anymore. He wanted to go home. He needed to find Elliot.

That's when Pete noticed the latch on the window that led outside.

* * *

Grace stood in the hallway, shaking her head. She was holding her compass, turning it over in her fingers while Sheriff Dentler, Deputy Smalls, and Doctor Marquez spoke in low tones.

"How's he doing?" the sheriff asked.

The doctor consulted a clipboard in his hands. "Pretty well, all things considered. No signs of malnourishment or serious exposure. He might have a bump on his head, but—"

"Lucky kid," Sheriff Dentler interrupted.

"Super lucky," Deputy Smalls added.

"I just don't get it," Grace said. "Where did he come from?"

The sheriff shrugged. "My guess? He was on a picnic or a camping trip. He wandered off from his family, got himself lost. . . ."

"But when?" Grace asked. "He looks like he's been out there for . . . who knows how long? And he had this. . . ."

Grace held up the compass.

Sheriff Dentler squinted at it. "You sure that's yours?"

Grace opened the compass to reveal the family

photo hidden inside. "Pretty sure," she said with a wry half-smile.

"Hmmm . . ." the sheriff mused. "We'll add that to the list of questions then. He's probably got a mom and dad out there somewhere, worried sick about him."

Just then, a nurse arrived, leading Natalie into the hallway. Her knee was bandaged, but she looked fine otherwise.

Grace placed her hands on Natalie's shoulders. "How are you feeling?"

"It was just a scrape," Natalie said. "Where's Pete?"

Grace gestured toward Pete's room. Natalie wandered over to peek through the window. Meanwhile, Grace turned to the doctor.

"I'm going to take Natalie home and then head back to the forest. Maybe there's something out there. A clue or something. Can you call me as soon as he wakes up?"

"Of course," said the doctor.

"Um, actually," Natalie interrupted them. She pointed into Pete's room. The window to the outside was wide open, curtains billowing in the breeze.

"He's gone," Natalie finished.

CHAPTER FOURTEEN

"I think we're lost, Gavin," the logger named Bobby announced.

Gavin shook his head. "Nah, I know where we're going."

The group of loggers-turned-hunters had been searching the woods for hours for the creature that had knocked over the tree. But they had nothing to show for it. No deer. No bears. No anything.

Up ahead, Woodrow and Abner suddenly stopped. "Hey! Come check this out!" Woodrow called.

The men hurried over to find Woodrow standing over a footprint. A *massive* footprint.

"What do you think?" Woodrow asked, kneeling down. "A bear?"

"You ever see a bear that big?" Gavin asked.

"I thought I did once," Bobby said. "Turned out it was just Abner's sister."

Abner punched Bobby in the arm as the men laughed. But suddenly, Gavin held up his hand. Something had moved in his peripheral vision. Something large . . .

But no . . . there was nothing there. . . .

Gavin squinted. "Do you all remember those stories Meacham used to tell us?"

"Oh, yeah!" Bobby said. "How's that song go?"

"*They come from the earth*," Abner started to sing off-key. "*They come from the stone . . .*"

"*Way up north, that's where they call home*," Bobby chimed in.

All the men joined the impromptu sing-along as they started to head deeper into the woods. "*Go where the mountains meet the sea. Look, look all around you . . .*"

Gavin muttered the last line under his breath. "*. . . there dragons will be.*"

CHAPTER FIFTEEN

Pete's bare feet flew across the concrete. All of Millhaven stretched out before him: the quaint little main street, buildings, and people coming and going.

Pete sprinted down the sidewalk, overwhelmed and dizzy. Everything was strange. From each direction something new assaulted Pete's senses.

He staggered and took a deep breath, then bellowed with all his might.

"ELLIOT!"

Pete turned a corner, almost running smack into a man and woman walking their small dog. It let out a high-pitched yip.

"Oh, my goodness!" the woman cried.

"Daphne, cut that out!" the man chastised the barking dog.

Pete knew what to do; his experience in the forest had taught him that much at least. Crouching down, he bared his teeth and barked back. The little dog stopped yipping in surprise.

Without missing a beat, Pete darted into the street.

SCREECH. A large car almost ran him over!

"Are you all right, son?" The driver started to get out of the car. "I almost—"

But Pete didn't want another adult to grab hold of him. He jumped onto the hood of the car and clambered right up and over it!

Meanwhile, a bright yellow school bus cruised down the other lane. Pete wasted no time. He leaped onto it, clinging to the back door. The wind cut through Pete's hair and made his strange new clothes billow. The bus was moving faster than he'd anticipated, but it wasn't anything he couldn't handle.

Pete started to climb to the top, suddenly noticing the kids shouting and pointing at him from inside the bus. One freckled kid stuck out his tongue. Pete stuck out his tongue right back at him. The kid clapped in delight.

Finally, Pete made it to the top of the moving school bus. He crouched down, finding his balance. The wind whipped his hair back. It was a strange sensation, not quite the same as flying with Elliot but not entirely different, either.

Pete stared as the buildings sped by. Over the rooftops he could see the smokestacks of the mill, and beyond that, the great green hills of the forest.

That was where he needed to be. That was where he would find Elliot.

Suddenly, a loud, high-pitched sound broke Pete's concentration. He looked around to see multiple police cars, sirens blaring, surrounding the bus.

The bus began to pull over. That was not good. As the vehicle slowed, Pete saw his only chance. In one smooth motion he leaped from the top of the bus to the roof of a car, and from there he hopped down to the ground. The children on the bus cheered, but Pete was already too far away to hear them.

As quickly as he could, Pete sprinted down the sidewalk and turned into an alley.

Dead end.

He whirled around, only to see two men—the sheriff and the deputy—blocking his exit.

Pete backed up and tried to climb the wall. But his hands slipped on the hard cement.

The men approached him. He was trapped.

And then, suddenly, he heard a voice.

"Pete."

He whirled around to see the redheaded lady with the silver disk. She was moving slowly toward him. He tried to make a break for it, but she stopped him, gently holding his shoulders and kneeling down to his eye level.

"We're not going to hurt you. Everything is okay. . . ."

Pete felt his throat tighten and tears started to well up in his eyes. Grace drew him in close. He felt overwhelmed and scared and out of his element, but something familiar about her touch and the way she spoke . . . it helped him relax.

"Just breathe deep," Grace said, stroking his hair. "Breathe. . . ." She demonstrated for him, taking a deep audible breath and letting it out.

Pete followed suit, exhaling rapidly.

"That's it. Just let it out," Grace encouraged.

And then Pete raised his head and let out a long and mournful howl.

CHAPTER SIXTEEN

Pete sat in the back of Grace's jeep, huddled in a corner on the floor behind the seat. He looked altogether miserable.

"It's okay, Pete," Grace said sympathetically. "You don't have to go back to the hospital. We're going somewhere much nicer. . . ."

"We're going to my house!" yelled Natalie from the front seat. Pete slowly lifted his head.

"Can I ask you a question, Pete?" Grace caught his eye in the rearview mirror and held up the silver disk. "Can you tell me how you came by this?"

With a hoarse whisper, Pete answered, "Where the trees ran away."

Natalie fiddled with a dial on the dashboard of the vehicle. As she turned it, there were crackling and hissing noises. Then, suddenly . . . music.

Music! Pete had forgotten music. The melody swept over him like a long-ago memory he didn't even know he'd lost. For the first time since he'd left the forest, he started to relax.

Grace stopped the car outside a large country home and opened the driver's side door.

"Come inside, Pete," Grace said, waving the boy toward the house. "Let's get you something to eat."

Pete shook his head. "I want to go home."

Grace crouched down next to him. "Where is your home?"

Pete just stared out toward the direction of the forest.

"Well," Grace said, "it's going to be dark soon. How about this: if you come with me now, I'll take you back there tomorrow and you can show me exactly where you live."

Pete paused. He didn't know what to say, but he was feeling odd. For some reason, his mind went back to the rabbit he had found the other day. The one that didn't bite him or scratch him as he held it. The rabbit knew he didn't mean any harm . . . and somehow he knew Grace didn't mean any harm, either.

"You know," Grace continued, "when I was a

little girl, I wanted to live in the forest more than anything. I loved being out there with the trees and the animals. So when I grew up, I made it my job to protect the woods and everything in them, which I suppose . . . includes you."

Pete looked at Grace. "And Elliot?" he asked.

"Elliot?" Grace replied. "Who's Elliot?"

CHAPTER SEVENTEEN

Meanwhile, deep in the woods, Gavin and the other three hunters stood awestruck.

"This is nuts. You think the kid did all this?" Woodrow asked.

The sun was setting and the hunters were staring at the massive tree house in front of them—Pete's tree house.

Gavin shook his head. Suddenly, something shiny caught his eye.

The missing keys from one of the backhoes.

"Well . . ." he muttered. "Someone's been living here. Or something."

Gavin made his way to the cave at the bottom of the tree house and peered inside. As his eyes adjusted to the dark, he spotted something on the cave floor just beyond the entrance. He stepped closer. It was . . . a storybook?

Gavin picked it up by the cover. Dirt and debris fell off the pages. And there, written clear as day on the inside cover of the book, was a name.

THIS BOOK BELONGS TO PETE.

Gavin hurried back to the other loggers. "Hey, guys, look at this."

ROOOAAAR!

The booming sound was enough to knock the loggers off their feet. Some enormous wild creature was roaring at them from inside the cave!

"Run!" Abner yelled.

Within moments, all four men were scrambling through the dense brush to reach their truck.

Three of them jumped in the front, and Gavin leaped into the bed of the truck, rifle in hand. Abner turned the key in the ignition.

But the truck wouldn't move.

The engine was running, but it seemed like a large force was holding it in place. The wheels spun wildly, dirt spraying from the tires as they turned uselessly against the ground. Then, without warning, the truck jerked upward. Gavin flew forward, his face smooshing against the glass of the rear window.

"It's gonna eat us!" Abner yelled.

Gavin peeled himself off the back window and looked over the side of the truck. The back wheels weren't touching the ground. How was that possible?

Suddenly, the bumper fell off the truck!

Gavin raised his rifle. Something was there. He just couldn't see it.

Before he could fire a shot, he was lifted high into the air, then dropped to the forest floor with a thud. The rifle landed beside him, its solid metal barrel bent like a candy cane, useless.

Gavin could hear a loud sniffing sound. He sat frozen in fear. Something was smelling him! Then . . .

"AHH-CHOO!" The thing let out a giant sneeze, blowing Gavin backward and covering him in sticky goo. And for just the briefest moment, Gavin caught a glimpse of Elliot's outline before the dragon vanished again.

Gavin scrambled away, jumping back in the truck with his fellow loggers. Abner stepped on the gas, and this time, the truck sped forward. As they drove away, Gavin could only whisper, "Did you see that? Did you see . . . ? That . . . was a dragon!"

High above them, virtually invisible in the night sky, Elliot followed.

CHAPTER EIGHTEEN

Pete sat at the dining room table inside Jack's comfortable and quiet house, wolfing down a peanut butter sandwich. Grace looked on, awestruck. It was as though the boy hadn't ever tasted anything so delicious.

Grace and Jack watched from the edge of the room as Natalie brought more and more food out for Pete.

"I wish you would have maybe called first . . ." Jack said to Grace, watching Pete pop the last bit of sandwich into his mouth.

Grace smiled. "I figured you wouldn't mind."

"Sure . . ." Jack answered. "But please tell me you at least told the sheriff?"

Grace tapped the badge of her ranger uniform.

"I *am* a government official, Jack. I do things by the book."

Jack laughed ruefully, and Grace took the jar of peanut butter from him to make Pete a second sandwich.

"I told the sheriff Pete can stay here just until we find out where he belongs," Grace said, spreading the thick peanut butter on the bread. "This is cozier than the hospital. And besides, maybe he'll open up more around someone his own age and tell us where he came from."

Grace watched Natalie share a cookie with Pete. Just as he had with the sandwich, the boy acted as if he was tasting a rare delicacy from a far-off land. Everything seemed so new, so foreign to him.

Suddenly, he stuffed multiple cookies in his mouth, making his cheeks puff out like a chipmunk's.

"How long has it been since you *ate*?" Natalie asked.

"Slow down there, buddy. It's gonna start coming out of your ears," Jack said, pushing a glass of water toward Pete. "Here, drink something."

Pete looked at the glass strangely, then lifted it and tipped the contents into his mouth all at once—messy but effective.

Jack laughed, rushing to grab a towel. Grace watched with a smile as Jack and Natalie cleaned up the mess. That was one thing she really liked about Jack. Despite their disagreements about the forest, he was a good man and a good dad.

Feeling her eyes on him, Jack looked up at Grace and grinned. "Gotta say: living in the woods, doing things his own way . . . sounds like he's a boy after your own heart."

* * *

An hour later, Pete was very full and very cozy. He had changed into some of Natalie's pajamas. They were sure a lot softer than the hospital clothes—and softer than anything he'd ever worn in the woods.

Pete wandered through the living room. Grace and Jack sat talking, and Natalie followed close behind him. Pete poked his fingers in the ashes filling the fireplace, making them black and sooty. He banged on the piano keys, enjoying the sounds. Then he meandered to a bookshelf. One very familiar book caught his eye—a pristine copy of *Elliot Gets Lost*. How did that get there?

Pulling it off the shelf, he began flipping through the pages.

"Oh," Natalie said, looking over his shoulder. "I haven't really read that book in forever. Someone gave that to me when I was learning to read, but now I read longer . . ."

Five-year-old Pete reads his favorite storybook, *Elliot Gets Lost,* in the backseat of his parents' car.

Mr. Meacham tells the local children about how he saw a dragon many years ago.

Pete's family's car crashes, and the little boy gets lost in the forest. There he meets . . . a dragon!

Six years after the car crash, Pete has grown up—and he and Elliot are each other's family!

Forest ranger Grace Meacham takes her job protecting the woods very seriously.

Pete finds Grace's compass in the woods. It is very intriguing.

Natalie spots Pete high up in a tree. She tells her father and Grace that she found a strange boy in the woods.

Grace and Jack take Pete into town, but Pete escapes. He has to find Elliot!

Pete leaps on top of a school bus, determined to make his way back to the forest.

Gavin and some other lumberjacks discover that Elliot is living in the forest, and they set out to trap him.

Elliot sees Pete with Jack, Natalie, and Grace. He thinks Pete has found a new family.

Jack reads Pete and Natalie a storybook. Pete feels very at home with them.

Pete takes some of his new friends to meet Elliot.

Now that everyone knows that Elliot is in the woods, Pete must make a choice.

Gavin captures Elliot, but Mr. Meacham, Pete, and Natalie
help the dragon escape!

Will Pete find his true family after all?

Natalie trailed off, a realization coming to her. "Elliot," she said, pointing toward the cover of the book.

At that word, Grace turned her head, just as the phone started to ring.

Pete jumped at the sound, startled.

"Hold your horses," Jack said, shooting the boy a smile. "It's just the telephone." He went to answer it as Grace moved over to Pete and Natalie, staring at the book.

"Is this Elliot?" she asked, pointing to the picture of the dog on the cover.

Pete shook his head.

Grace tried again. "Is Elliot a person?"

"No."

"Is he an animal? Like a dog or a cat?"

After thinking a moment, Pete shook his head. "Uh-uh."

"What is he—"

"Grace?" Jack interrupted them, a grim expression on his face. "It's the sheriff. He wants to talk to you."

Grace turned to Natalie, sharing a quick look with her. "Natalie, why don't you take Pete up to your room for a minute?"

CHAPTER NINETEEN

Natalie guided Pete upstairs to her room. Whatever the grown-ups were talking about, it definitely had to do with Pete, and it didn't seem good.

The boy hesitated before stepping into her room. The white walls and traces of pink on the curtains and bed seemed to throw him.

"It's okay . . ." Natalie said. "We can color. Do you like to color?"

Pete shrugged.

A few minutes later, it was clear that Pete did like to color. *A lot.* He was sitting on the floor completely engrossed in his artwork. He gripped a crayon tightly in his fist, drawing green markings across a piece of paper.

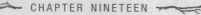

"Pete, is Elliot your imaginary friend?" Natalie asked, sitting down at the foot of her bed and watching him.

"What's 'imaginary'?" Pete asked without looking up from the paper.

Natalie paused before answering. "It's . . . it's when you make something up in your head so that you have someone to talk to and keep you from being lonely."

Pete kept coloring, but it was clear he was thinking about the question.

Finally, he spoke. "Are they funny?"

"Sure," Natalie answered.

"Can they fly?" Pete asked.

Natalie shrugged. "I guess they can do whatever you want them to. That's what makes them imaginary."

Pete looked up at Natalie. "Are you my imaginary friend, too?"

Natalie shook her head. "I'm real."

"Oh," Pete said. "Then so is Elliot."

Pete put the finishing touches on his drawing. Natalie leaned over to see it. It was a simple but crystal-clear image of a little boy and a big green dragon.

"I have to get back to him," Pete whispered. "He gets scared when I'm gone."

Natalie examined the drawing, unsure of what to say. She gave him another piece of paper, and he started to draw another picture of a dragon.

"Does Elliot have any parents?" Natalie asked.

Pete shrugged, focusing on his drawing. "Can't find them. We looked. Inside rocks, up in the sky, under trees . . ."

"Oh," Natalie said, remembering something. "It's like the song?"

Pete stopped drawing. "What song?"

Natalie paused for a minute, trying to remember the lyrics. She started to sing in a soft, sweet voice:

> Go north, go north,
> With wings on your feet,
> Go north with the wind
> Where the three rivers meet.
> Now plant yourself down
> beside the tallest tree.
> Measure the stars shining
> one, two, three.
> Look all around you and see,
> Deep in the forest, there dragons will be.

* * *

At the same moment, not far from Natalie's comfortable bedroom, Elliot landed with a heavy thud on one of the great smokestacks of the mill just outside the forest. He looked toward the twinkling lights of the town and let out a long and mournful howl.

But there was no response.

Elliot didn't know where Pete was, but the dragon had smelled Pete's scent on the strange man in the forest. And he'd followed him.

Elliot watched the man's truck speeding toward town below him. Then the dragon lifted off the smokestack and flapped his mighty wings to continue following it.

A short while later, the truck drove past the hospital where Grace and the others had first taken Pete. Elliot had no way of knowing this. But he could smell faint whiffs of Pete's scent in the air around the hospital. He landed on the roof with a heavy *thud*.

At the nurse's station, great puffs of dust drifted down from the ceiling. In an examination room, a doctor looked curiously at her instruments rattling on the tray. And in a hospital room, a young girl with a broken leg sat in bed watching TV with her mother. Elliot's large upside-down face peered through the window.

The mother didn't notice. But the little girl did. She giggled and waved.

Elliot snorted. No Pete.

He'd have to keep following the scent.

He'd have to keep looking.

CHAPTER TWENTY

"I can drop him off on my way to the mill tomorrow," Jack said. His expression was somber, just like Grace's.

They were standing in the kitchen discussing what Sheriff Dentler had told them on the phone. The sheriff had figured out Pete's identity. A missing child report had been filed six years earlier—after the night of the fateful car crash.

The report indicated that Pete had no living relatives. So Sheriff Dentler had arranged for Child Protective Services to take Pete into custody in the morning. Grace and Jack just had to drop him off at the station.

"No, no—I'll do it," Grace told Jack, her mind reeling. "I just . . ."

Everything was happening so quickly. Grace had thought they'd have time to unravel Pete's story. Now, suddenly, he was being taken away. There were too many questions that still needed answers.

Jack reached out to touch her arm. "Just what?"

"Six years, Jack! How could he have survived? Through the cold and the snow?"

"Kids are stronger than we think," Jack said.

"I know, but he was out there for so long, and I never saw him once." Grace sank into a chair.

Jack sat down next to her. "Well, I think it's safe to say that there's more out there than any of us will ever see. You're lucky you found him. And so is he."

* * *

A few minutes later, as Grace was heading upstairs to check on Pete and Natalie, the doorbell rang.

Jack went to open the door, and his brother burst in. Gavin seemed frazzled, his hair disheveled and his face pale. He immediately checked the peephole to see whether he had been followed.

"Gavin?" Jack asked. "What's going on?"

Gavin peered through the blinds and out the window.

"There's something out there, Jack. In the woods. Something big, and dangerous. It almost killed us—"

"Oh, my god!" exclaimed Jack. "Are you okay?"

Gavin continued as if he hadn't heard his brother. "That kid, he knows what it is. Is he here? Is Pete here?"

Jack was even more confused. "Yes. But—"

Gavin interrupted him. "We've got to sit him down! We've gotta ask him just what it is we're dealing with—"

"Hold on, hold on. Calm down," Jack said. "Ask him about what?"

Gavin was pacing the room. "You remember those stories? The ones Grace's dad used to tell all the kids?"

"About a dragon in the forest?" Jack asked. "Yeah. Why?"

Gavin looked straight at his brother. "I don't think he was making them up."

For a moment, Jack didn't say anything. Then he furrowed his brow. "You sure you weren't just seeing things?"

"For crying out loud, Jack! I'm lucky to be alive right now! I know what I saw. And if we go out there, the two of us, if we can catch this thing—we're not going to have to worry about the mill anymore. We'll be rich!"

Now Jack was starting to feel annoyed. Even when his brother seemed scared half to death, his mind always went back to money. Always.

Gavin must have sensed his brother's irritation because he stopped trying to convince him. He moved to go upstairs. Jack stepped in front of him, blocking the path.

"Let me just see Pete. Okay?" Gavin said. "I just need to talk to him."

"No, Gavin," Jack said firmly. "Not tonight."

"But—" Gavin insisted, moving to step past his brother.

Jack blocked him again. "Here's what we're going to do: you get some sleep. Tomorrow, meet me at the mill and you and I will go out to those woods. We'll get Grace and the rangers to come with us."

"Aw, come on . . ."

Jack shook his head. "If there's something out there, we'll find it. Together. We'll do things right for once."

Gavin frowned. "You don't believe me, do you?"

"I want to, Gavin." Jack sighed. "But sometimes you make it pretty hard."

Gavin's face flared red. "Okay. Fine. I get the picture." And with that, he angrily stormed out of the house.

"Gavin . . ." Jack called. But it was too late. His brother was already gone.

* * *

As Gavin's truck sped into the distance away from the house, Elliot quietly emerged from the dense brush.

The dragon's green fur shone under the moonlight. He looked at Jack's house distrustfully, as if it were another animal. With a sniff of caution, the large dragon took a step forward.

Suddenly, a hissing sound came out of nowhere, startling Elliot. He jumped back and then growled at the source of the noise.

It was a lawn sprinkler. It had turned on. But to Elliot, it looked like a tiny glowing creature that sprayed water on the grass.

The dragon narrowed his eyes and padded forward, waiting for just the right time to strike. The glowing creature was small, yes. But Elliot could tell that it was a dangerous enemy. And so the dragon bided his time until . . .

BOOM!

Elliot pounced, landing on the sprinkler with all his weight. Victory! The sprinkler had never stood a chance, and its evil water-spraying ways were forever put to rest.

Now Elliot had to get back to finding Pete.

CHAPTER TWENTY-ONE

Inside the house, Grace gently knocked on the door to Natalie's room.

"Hey, you two," Grace said, opening the door. "Natalie, do you think I could talk to Pete alone for a minute?"

"Sure." Natalie hopped off the bed. She gave Pete a reassuring look before leaving the room.

Grace knelt near Pete, who was sitting by the window. Outside, trees swayed in the wind.

"Pete," Grace asked gently. "Do you remember how you got lost in the woods?"

Pete thought for a moment. His expression darkened as the memories returned to him.

"It was a long time ago, wasn't it?" Grace asked, reaching out and stroking the young boy's hair.

Pete nodded. "We were on an adventure."

His words sent a pang through Grace's heart. She couldn't imagine how hard it had been for the poor boy. How hard life had been for all those years on his own. "You know, Pete . . ." Grace fidgeted, working to find the words. "I lost my mother when I wasn't much older than you. I know how hard it can be. But you should know—you're not alone."

Pete looked at Grace. "I know."

"You do?" Grace asked.

Pete nodded. "I have Elliot."

Grace paused. She needed to get to the bottom of this. "Who is Elliot? Can you tell me more about him?"

Pete walked over to Natalie's desk and cleared away the crayons he had left out. Underneath was his drawing, which he carefully picked up and handed to Grace.

"For me?" she asked.

Pete nodded and Grace looked down at the drawing.

"That's Elliot," Pete said.

Grace was stunned. Whatever she had thought Elliot was, it wasn't that. She felt her heart leap into her throat. The drawing was . . . familiar.

Grace cleared her throat. "He must . . . he must be a very special friend."

Pete nodded. "When I go back tomorrow you can see him."

Grace stared at Pete, who was looking at her with large, hopeful eyes. In the course of the past few minutes, he had opened up so much. And tomorrow she was supposed to drop him off at Child Protective Services, to be shuffled out into the system. She would probably never see him again.

Unable to bring herself to say otherwise, Grace nodded and said the gentlest thing she could think of. "Tomorrow . . . we'll get you back where you belong."

Pete's face lit up with joy. He reached out and hugged Grace.

Grace barely knew how to react, her own guilt weighing heavily on her. Instead of saying anything, she hugged him back.

"Okay," Grace said finally. "Let's get you to bed."

"Can we read my story?" Pete asked hopefully.

Grace tilted her head. "What's your story?" she asked.

* * *

Unbeknownst to Pete, Elliot was quietly lumbering up to the house at that exact moment. He stepped as lightly as a giant green dragon with the power of camouflage possibly could.

Elliot bent down, his large snout almost touching the wet ground at the base of the house. Pete's scent was stronger than ever. He had to be there! Elliot peered in a window. No Pete. He looked through another one. Still no Pete.

Moving quietly around the side of the house, the dragon craned his neck to peek through a third window. His eyes grew wide. There was Pete! He had found him!

The dragon was about to howl happily. But then he stopped. What he saw was . . . confusing.

Pete was sitting on a foldout couch, snuggled up with other humans—a little girl and a man. The woman with the red hair from the day before was standing by the window, watching them with a warm smile.

The man held a book on his lap, reading aloud. "'This is the story of a little puppy. His name is—'"

"Elliot," Pete finished.

Elliot's ears perked up. That was how Pete's storybook started. The man was reading their story!

The man continued. "'He is going on an adventure with his family. They are going—'"

"Wait," Pete interrupted. "This isn't how it is when I tell it."

"Do you want me to stop?" the man asked.

Pete thought about it for a moment, then shook his head. "No. I like it."

Elliot watched as Pete smiled and snuggled deeper into the cushions, sandwiched between the other humans. He looked . . . happy.

Elliot's face fell. Pete had found a new story and a new home.

His head hanging, the dragon turned away from the window and began the long trek back to his cave—alone.

CHAPTER TWENTY-TWO

Much later that night, Grace pushed her way through the piles of papers on her father's desk. She was searching for something very important.

Mr. Meacham's workstation was cluttered with old newspaper clippings and photos of strange animal footprints. With one hand Grace moved the lamp, the light drifting over a map covered in red pins that supposedly signified dragon sightings.

"Can I help you find something?"

Grace jumped at the sound of her father's voice.

"Sorry," she said, rubbing her temples. "I thought you were asleep."

"Nah," he answered. "What's on your mind?"

"Well . . ." She wondered how she could broach the subject with her father. It was probably best just to come right out with it. "Did you hear about Pete? That boy we found in the woods?"

"Oh, sure," her father replied. "The whole town's been buzzing about him."

Grace held out the drawing Pete had made—the drawing of Elliot. "He drew this."

Mr. Meacham looked at the picture. His face paled.

"Pete says this is his friend," Grace continued. "From the forest. And it reminded me of—"

"Oh," her father said, nodding, "I know what it reminded you of."

Mr. Meacham reached under a pile of papers and tugged out one particular sheet, revealing an old, yellowed drawing—one of a dragon that looked remarkably similar to Pete's.

"This one," Mr. Meacham finished, handing the drawing to his daughter.

"How old was I?" Grace asked. "When you drew this for me?"

Her father shrugged. "Five? Six? It was before your mother passed away, I know that much."

"But . . ." she whispered. "But it was always just a story."

Mr. Meacham shook his head. "It was never just a story."

"But none of it was real!" Grace insisted. "You

change it every time you tell it! And your scars—those are from a bear trap you fell into when you were ten. Mom told me!"

"I may have embellished a few things here and there," Mr. Meacham said. "But tales, they're always better when they're tall. It was a long time ago, and everyone thinks I'm crazy. Lord knows there have been days where I wonder if they're right. But then I think about the magic. Maybe I'll never see that dragon again, but just knowing it's out there . . ."

Mr. Meacham flipped through the stack of pages on his desk.

"Well, it helps me see everything differently. The trees. The sunshine. Even you. And I wouldn't trade that for anything in the world."

Grace felt her throat tighten as her father continued.

"I'm not going to try to convince you to believe me," he said. "I quit that. But maybe you should be open to looking."

Grace shook her head. "I know those woods like the back of my hand. I couldn't have missed a dragon."

Mr. Meacham focused on his daughter, his eyes seeming to see right through her.

"You missed Pete."

CHAPTER TWENTY-THREE

Pete was sound asleep.

A hand brushed across his forehead, pushing back his long hair. With some effort, he opened his eyes.

Grace was kneeling by his bedside. "Good morning . . ." she said with a warm smile.

Pete returned her smile. He felt happy. He had new friends. And best of all, he was going to get to share those new friends with Elliot!

Once Pete was up, Jack helped him put on some new clothes. Soon Pete was chasing Natalie down the stairs and out the front door. The excitement he felt was almost overwhelming.

Pete, Natalie, and Grace climbed into the jeep. Jack reached in through the window and tousled Pete's hair.

"All right, Pete. You take care, okay? Be well."

Pete grinned in response. He was going home to Elliot. How could he not be well? He would be the best!

Jack made his way to the driver's side and talked quietly with Grace.

"I've gotta run up to the mill and see Gavin," Jack said. "Call me if you need anything, okay?"

Grace waved away his concern. "We'll be fine!" she said, giving him a quick kiss on the cheek.

Grace looked back at Pete in the rearview mirror, gave him an encouraging grin, and then they were off.

* * *

But Grace didn't feel nearly as happy as she appeared.

Nothing about what she was supposed to do felt right. Taking Pete to Child Protective Services . . . lying to him when he trusted her . . .

And then there was the matter of the dragon. Her father's dragon.

Grace thought back to the years of her father telling her the stories of the forest—stories that had inspired her to become the person she was.

She slowly approached the sheriff's station. There was a car parked out front with a CHILD PROTECTIVE SERVICES logo on it.

Grace felt her stomach lurch. There really was only one choice she could make.

She kept on driving past the station, making the turn toward her father's house.

"Pete . . ." Grace said. "There's someone I want to come with us—someone who knows the woods better than I do."

CHAPTER TWENTY-FOUR

A quiet day was progressing at the mill. It was the weekend, and only a handful of workers were on-site. That didn't mean there wasn't a lot to do. The warehouse was open and empty, waiting on a load of wood from up north. The yard was filled with trucks and cars, several of which should have been out in the forest with work crews. Gavin was supposed to be overseeing everything—but he wasn't there. Jack stopped one of the mill workers. "Have you seen Gavin?" he asked.

The worker shrugged. "He and Woodrow got some of the guys together and took a truck out to the new cutdown."

Jack raised his eyebrows. "What for?"

"He said they were going to do some hunting," the worker replied.

Jack suddenly had a bad feeling in the pit of his stomach.

He hurried into his office to call his brother. He found a note on the desk. In his brother's scribbled handwriting, it read, *Gonna do something right for once.*

Just then, the telephone rang.

"Hello?" Jack answered.

"Hey, Jack." It was the sheriff. "Didn't you say Grace was planning on bringing Pete by today?"

"Yeah . . ." Jack said, his sense of unease growing. "She left an hour ago."

"Well, she hasn't shown up yet, and Carl at the ranger station said he saw her jeep heading out to the woods . . ." the sheriff replied.

Jack began to put the pieces together. He hung up the phone and ran out of his office as fast as he could.

CHAPTER TWENTY-FIVE

Pete leaped out of the jeep and bounded into the forest.

"This way!" the boy yelled excitedly.

Natalie ran after him as Grace and her father climbed out of the vehicle.

"Kids!" Grace yelled. "Hold on a second. . . ."

Natalie stopped, but Pete was already out of sight. He had even kicked off his shoes and left them on the grass.

Grace, Natalie, and Mr. Meacham hurried after the boy. After a few minutes, they stopped, looking around.

"I've never seen this part of the forest before," Grace said in a surprised voice.

Her father, however, gazed around in wonder. It was clear *he* had.

Suddenly, Pete reappeared from out of the thick brush.

"Come on!" he yelled. "This way!"

Grace, Natalie, and Mr. Meacham followed Pete as best they could, but it was difficult for anyone unfamiliar with the path. Pete led them through the bushes and under branches and around large rocks, until eventually . . .

They stood in front of Pete's sanctuary—his tree house.

Natalie gaped in awe. "You did this all yourself?" she asked.

Pete shook his head. "Elliot helped. I think he's hiding."

Softly, the boy called into the cave at the base of the tree house. "Elliot? You in there? Come on out!"

For a long moment there was no response. Grace and Natalie exchanged glances. But Mr. Meacham just waited, watching intently.

Then . . . a deep shuddering whimper echoed from within the dark cave. A chill ran down Grace's spine. Whatever that noise was, she had felt it deep in her bones.

Pete looked worried. "I'll go get him," the boy said.

Grace hesitated, uncertain, but then she stepped forward. "Pete, wait . . ." she called. But the boy had already disappeared into the depths of the cave.

So they waited.

Grace was growing more nervous. "I'm going in after him," she whispered. But her father reached out to hold her back.

"Just wait. Give him a second," he said.

And then there was a heaving rumble, like a boulder being moved. Pete reappeared. Natalie started to say something, but Pete shook his head and held a finger to his mouth.

"Shhh . . ." he said.

From the darkness behind Pete, Elliot emerged—completely visible to all.

Natalie's jaw dropped. So did Grace's. Her whole world had suddenly changed. Everything she had ever heard from her father—every story, every tall tale, all the things she had so long before dismissed as fiction—suddenly became real.

"Dad?" she asked, taking a step back.

Mr. Meacham beamed.

"It's okay, Grace," he said softly, keeping his

eyes on the large furry dragon. "Just as magnificent as I remember."

"You always said it was dangerous," Grace whispered.

In response, Elliot stretched up to his full height, giving them a friendly growl. Natalie stepped forward.

"Elliot?" she said.

Elliot purred more deeply. Natalie held up a shaking hand and ran it through Elliot's soft green fur. For a moment, it seemed like the dragon might sneeze. Then he blinked and snuggled his large face against the young girl.

Grace burst out laughing. Mr. Meacham joined in.

Pete smiled widely. Everything was going perfectly.

And that's when the gunshot echoed through the forest.

CHAPTER TWENTY-SIX

Everything turned to chaos.

At the sound of the blast, Elliot instantly drew backward, stung. A dart was protruding from his shoulder. The dragon dropped to all fours and bared his teeth like an angry lion. He stood in front of Pete, his wings flaring out protectively.

Gavin slid down the ridge with his hunting rifle in his hands. Behind him were several other loggers, all equally armed.

"Gavin, wait!" Mr. Meacham cried. But his voice was drowned out by Elliot, who bellowed a mighty roar so loud that the trees shook and several of the loggers stumbled to the ground.

Instinctively, Grace pushed Natalie behind her and reached for Pete. Not understanding Grace's actions, Elliot responded with a protective lunge, guarding Pete in turn. Then the dragon turned and roared at two of the loggers.

Both men fired their dart guns at the dragon. A silver dart whizzed through the air and struck, tearing a small hole in the membrane of Elliot's wing. The dragon roared in pain and reared up on his hind legs. Another dart struck in the middle of Elliot's chest.

Pete was beside himself. He screamed at the loggers to stop hurting his friend. But they weren't listening. Instead, they whipped a lasso around the dragon's neck.

Crack! Another shot from Gavin's rifle rang out. Elliot dodged the dart and, in doing so, yanked the lasso out of the logger's hands. The rope snagged on a tree branch, tearing the limb down. It barely missed Mr. Meacham as it fell.

"Hit him with all you got!" yelled one of the loggers.

Elliot flailed helplessly as the loggers continued to tie him up. Pete grabbed a stick and ran at the hunters. But Mr. Meacham caught Pete by the shoulders and held him back.

"Let me go! Let me *go!*" Pete cried, hysterical.

Another hunter grabbed one of the loose ropes that bound the dragon. But he failed to notice the trip wire from the trap that Pete had created a few days earlier. The trap's big log swung down and slammed into the hunter, sending him and his gun flying.

Pete realized this was Elliot's only chance.

"Fly, Elliot! *Fly!*" Pete yelled.

Elliot understood. He beat his wings and rose into the air. For a moment, it looked like it was going to work! The loggers lost hold of the ropes. Elliot soared higher. He was going to make it!

And then, all at once, the tranquilizers kicked in. Elliot grew woozy. His fur rippled, changing colors sporadically. His wings beat slower, and his eyelids drooped. With a tremendous groan, the dragon plummeted out of the sky, crashing into the tree house. Along with the dragon, the mighty structure collapsed to the ground.

"ELLIOT!" Pete cried. He finally broke free of Mr. Meacham's hold and ran to the collapsed dragon. Elliot was still breathing, but his eyes were closed.

Natalie was sobbing. Grace took a step toward Pete, but the boy could not be comforted. Not by her. He glared up at Grace, his eyes accusing her of betrayal. And then the little boy howled, burying his face in Elliot's fur.

Pete could hear Elliot's heartbeat deep within

the dragon's chest, strong at first but growing fainter and fainter. *He has to be okay, he has to be okay.* . . . The thought repeated in Pete's mind over and over.

Just then, Jack screeched up in his jeep. He looked on at the chaos: loggers scrambling; Natalie in tears; Grace and her father pale; and Pete sobbing, his face buried in the green fur of an impossible creature . . . a dragon.

Jack was at a loss for words.

"Gavin?" he asked, turning to his brother.

Everyone looked up, noticing Jack for the first time.

"Daddy?" Natalie said.

"What is this?" Jack asked in disbelief.

"This?" Gavin said triumphantly. "This is the Millhaven Dragon, and I caught it!"

CHAPTER TWENTY-SEVEN

The forest was quiet. Unusually so.

Pete sat in a corner of Jack's office on the second story of the mill building. A blanket was wrapped around his shoulders. Natalie was sitting in a chair next to him, looking straight ahead.

On the other side of a glass partition, Jack paced, holding his phone between his ear and shoulder. The glass was thick enough that the children could only hear Jack speaking in low, urgent tones—but they couldn't make out what he was saying. After several moments and a few phone calls, he hung up the phone and stepped into his main office, taking in Pete's stony expression.

"Natalie, can you sit tight with Pete for a minute?" he asked.

"What's going to happen to Elliot?" Natalie asked in reply.

"I don't know, sweetheart." Jack sighed, patting her head. "I'm going to find out. Stay right here, okay?"

Natalie nodded. But before he left, Jack looked sincerely at Pete. "Pete, we'll fix this. I promise," he said. Then he left Natalie and Pete alone in the office.

"Grace didn't mean for this to happen," Natalie whispered to Pete.

Pete turned away, looking out the window and across the mill yard to a large lumber warehouse. It had huge wooden double doors and a large skylight on the roof. Gavin and his friends stood outside the doorway to the warehouse, keeping guard. Elliot was in there, strapped with chains to a giant truck bed, unconscious.

Pete was heartbroken. How could he have let his friend down?

* * *

Inside the warehouse, Grace and her father stood next to the truck that held the sleeping dragon. Neither of them felt comfortable leaving Elliot alone with Gavin or the other loggers.

"How could I have never seen this until now? I feel like I'm dreaming," Grace said mournfully.

"I know the feeling," Mr. Meacham said, with a sad look in his eyes.

They stared at the massive beast. Elliot's fur looked very pale—sickly, like dried grass.

Gavin walked up behind them, whistling. "She's a beauty, isn't she? Or he. Or whatever it is." The logger glanced at Mr. Meacham. "Everyone thought you were crazy all these years, but not me. No, sir! I always believed you!"

Mr. Meacham just shook his head. "To be honest, I kinda wish you hadn't believed me."

Gavin rolled his eyes. "Are you kidding? You're lucky we got there when we did. He'd have eaten every last one of you!"

"He wasn't going to hurt anyone," Mr. Meacham responded. "And besides, now that you've got him, what exactly do you plan to do with him?"

Gavin suddenly looked uncertain.

"You don't know, do you?" Mr. Meacham pressed.

"I've got some ideas," Gavin snapped. "This dragon's gonna put me on the map, I can tell you that much. Folks will line up for miles to see this thing."

Elliot shuddered. His eye opened slightly—just enough to see Grace, and for Grace to see her own reflection in the glassy surface of Elliot's dark pupil.

Suddenly, Elliot was awake. He strained against his chains.

Two of the loggers whipped up their tranquilizer guns. Grace yelled at them, waving them down. "Wait! Wait," she said.

It hadn't mattered. Elliot was too weak to break the chains. He opened his mouth and let out a long, grievous moan—a deep earthly bellow full of pain and sadness. It was enough to shake the whole warehouse.

"Something's wrong," Grace said, worried. "I think the tranquilizer darts have made him sick."

"He's just sleepy," Gavin said with an unconcerned shrug. "We pumped him full of enough juice to keep him out for days."

"No, really. There's something wrong!" Grace insisted. "Just look at him. He needs help. He needs Pete."

At the sound of his friend's name, Elliot let out another low moan. In response, Grace reached out and gently stroked the large dragon's paw—a comforting touch. And just like when she'd comforted Pete in the alley, Grace's touch seemed to calm the dragon. The color of his fur began to shift where she'd touched him, matching Grace's skin tone. Then it turned back to green. Grace couldn't believe what she was seeing. She stared at the dragon in amazement.

Elliot raised his head and howled once more.

* * *

The sound echoed throughout the entire mill yard, reaching Pete and Natalie in Jack's office. Pete clenched his fists, feeling a lurch in the pit of his stomach. "What are they doing to him?"

"They're trying to figure out what he is and where he came from," Natalie said.

"He came from the woods," Pete said, "just like me. Why can't they just let us go?"

Natalie shook her head. "Because they're grown-ups."

There were tears in Pete's eyes. "What if he dies? We can tell them . . . ?"

"They won't listen," Natalie said bitterly. "We're just kids and they think they know better. They think they know how the whole world works and there's nothing we can do. Unless . . ."

Natalie's eyes flashed with an idea. She looked out the window.

"What if *we* rescued Elliot?"

CHAPTER TWENTY-EIGHT

Sirens suddenly blared through the afternoon air. Gavin glared at Jack. "Are you kidding me? You called the sheriff?"

"What did you expect me to do, Gavin?" Jack asked. "Keep it a secret?"

Gavin didn't answer; instead he stomped out of the warehouse angrily. Jack and Grace followed, closing the large doors behind them. By that time, the warehouse was surrounded by deputies and mill workers.

"Come to take a gander, Sheriff?" Gavin asked, smiling at both officers.

"Lots of crazy rumors flying around, Gavin," Sheriff Dentler answered. "What is it that's so big I had to see it for myself?"

Gavin held up a finger for emphasis. "Let me just say one thing first. What I'm about to show you . . . it belongs to me. I caught it fair and square, so whatever anyone tells you . . ." Gavin shot Grace a look. "It's mine."

During Gavin's rant, Grace was the only one to notice a sprinkle of sawdust drift down from the roof of the warehouse. She looked up . . . just in time to see something—or someone—disappear into the building.

* * *

Pete and Natalie climbed into the ventilation shaft, moving carefully on their hands and knees. It was a precarious path, but it seemed like it would hold. When they reached the rafters of the warehouse, they carefully climbed a steel ladder to the ground.

Pete gasped, taking in the horrible sight of his friend chained to the truck. He rushed over to the dragon.

"I'm sorry," Pete said, patting Elliot's fur gently. "We're gonna get you out of here."

Elliot let out a small purr, trying to lift his head to see his friend better. Pete continued to murmur to him in a soothing voice as he examined the chains that held the dragon down. He climbed onto the truck and pulled at them, finding enough slack to start pushing them free from the dragon.

Natalie moved to help him, but the sound of voices outside grabbed her attention. She tiptoed across the warehouse to the large closed doors. Her dad, Gavin, and the loggers were right outside. And it sounded like the police had arrived, too. Thinking fast, she slid a heavy crossbar into place across the door, locking it from the inside.

The voices got louder. Suddenly, the doors shook. Gavin started banging against them.

"Um, Pete?" Natalie called, trying to hold the crossbar in place.

Pete pulled the last chain off the dragon and eyed the large skylight above. It looked just about big enough for Elliot to fit through.

"Elliot, can you fly?" Pete asked his friend.

Elliot tried to stand, but he was too weak. His injured wing hung limply at his side.

Pete looked over at Natalie and the wooden doors. They were shaking violently—the adults were going to force their way in.

Pete and Natalie would have to think of another mode of escape . . . and quick.

CHAPTER TWENTY-NINE

"Hey!" Gavin yelled from outside the door. "Who's in there? Open up!"

Gavin flagged over some of the loggers, and soon they were pulling and prying at the doors with heavy tools. It took only a few minutes before the wooden crossbar started to break. It splintered and the door burst open. Gavin, the police, and all the loggers piled into the warehouse. What they saw made them gasp.

The flatbed was empty. The dragon was gone!

The sheriff frowned. "I don't see anything," he said.

"He was here!" Gavin exclaimed. "He was right here!"

"What was?" the sheriff asked.

"The . . . the dragon! Tell him, Jack!" Gavin sputtered.

"Dragon?" The sheriff was starting to sound annoyed. "Fellas, you dragged me all the way out here for this?"

Gavin shook his head. "It got out! Come on—we've gotta catch it before it gets too far!"

"Before what gets too far?" the sheriff asked. "Just tell me what I'm supposed to be looking for!"

"It's a dragon! It looks like a dragon!" Gavin yelled.

Meanwhile, Grace was studying the flatbed. How had Elliot escaped? They had been right outside the warehouse and hadn't heard anything.

Suddenly, she noticed a small movement on the far side of the warehouse. Grace waited until Gavin and the others had stormed back outside, still arguing. Then she moved around toward the back of the truck. She bent down to find Pete's face staring out at her from behind one of the front tires.

Pete's eyes shifted nervously. And that was when she noticed it. A faint shimmer above the flatbed, like a ripple in the air. Elliot hadn't escaped at all. He was still right there, just camouflaged!

Grace looked back at Pete and gave him a wink. She wouldn't let him down this time. Quietly, she headed outside to join the others and closed the large doors behind her.

Amidst the hubbub outside, Grace pulled Jack aside. "Jack! It's still here! The dragon is still here! We've got to do something!"

Meanwhile, back inside the warehouse, the air shimmered and shifted. Elliot reappeared. He had done his best to stay completely invisible, and the effort had left him exhausted.

"How do we get him out of here?" Natalie asked Pete.

Pete eyed the truck. "Do you know how to drive?"

Natalie clambered up into the truck's cab. "Sort of. But my dad's truck doesn't have this many handles."

Suddenly, someone spoke behind the two children.

"Your feet can't even reach the pedals. Scoot over." It was Mr. Meacham. He must have stayed in the warehouse when everyone else had left!

Both children hesitated, uncertain.

"I don't want to hurt your friend, kids," Mr. Meacham promised. "I just want to help."

Pete looked at Natalie, and she nodded. They could trust the old man. Within seconds, the two kids shifted over and Mr. Meacham climbed into the driver's seat. He took the pocketknife he carried around—the one he liked to use to add dramatic flair to his stories—and jammed it into the ignition of the car. He turned it hard, starting the engine.

"Better buckle up," Mr. Meacham said with a glint in his eye.

He slammed on the gas and the truck barreled through the wooden doors of the warehouse, obliterating them.

CHAPTER THIRTY

As the truck carrying the great green dragon burst out of the warehouse, the sheriff wheeled in surprise.

"That's . . . that's not . . . real . . . is it?" he stammered.

The truck barreled toward the gates of the mill yard. Everyone watched in shock as Mr. Meacham crashed it through the gates and drove at top speed into the forest. On the back of the fleeing vehicle was Elliot, clinging to the flatbed for dear life.

Gavin was the first to snap out of it. "Everyone after them!" he cried.

Thinking quickly, Grace snatched Gavin's car keys out of his hand and tossed them into the nearby bushes. That would slow him down.

"Sorry about that!" she yelled over her shoulder as she and Jack raced for their pickup.

Gavin fumed. There was no way he was letting anyone steal his dragon! He found his keys and stormed after the others.

With that, the yard was full of engines revving and vehicles streaming out of the mill yard and into the forest in hot pursuit.

* * *

Mr. Meacham drove madly down the rough road, occasionally catching air. The mud flaps slapped loudly against the back bumper. On the bed of the truck, Elliot hung tight, a hint of his old color returning as the group made their daring escape. A cavalcade of smaller vehicles was gaining ground rapidly behind them. Jack's pickup was in the lead, and Gavin's was close behind.

Gavin's vehicle suddenly surged ahead, passing Jack and Grace dangerously on the narrow dirt road. Several police cars and other emergency vehicles followed, their sirens blaring.

Pete looked out the back window to see Gavin's car gaining on them.

"Faster!" Pete yelled.

"I'm working on it!" Mr. Meacham cried.

The truck rattled and shook. Mr. Meacham pushed down on the gas pedal, getting every bit of thrust the engine had left in it. With a burst of speed, they surged downhill toward a narrow bridge up ahead.

Pete looked back at his friend, who was nestled down, clinging to the flatbed. Elliot needed Pete to be brave, so he would be.

Suddenly, Gavin's truck seemed to kick into a higher gear. His engine roared and he swerved up ahead of them, cutting off the semi. But instead of stopping, Gavin continued speeding toward the bridge. At the last possible moment, he slammed on his brakes, fishtailing to a halt and blocking the road ahead.

"*Ahhh!*" Pete and Natalie screamed as they barreled toward his truck.

Just then, Gavin climbed out of the vehicle, waving at them to stop.

"That fool's out of his mind!" Mr. Meacham cried. He had no choice; he couldn't run over Gavin. He slammed on the brakes. But the wheels locked up, and the truck's momentum kept it sliding forward at breakneck speed.

"No! Do something!" Natalie cried as the truck bore down on her uncle.

"I'm trying!" yelled Mr. Meacham.

But there was nowhere for the truck to go—nowhere but straight across the bridge. And Mr. Meacham realized that if he kept trying to stop the vehicle, they would just crash right off the side into the deep ravine below.

So instead, Mr. Meacham did the only thing he really *could* do. He slammed on the gas and leaned on the horn, barreling straight toward Gavin.

"He's . . . he's not that crazy . . ." Gavin muttered uncertainly, lifting up a hand, as if that would stop the enormous vehicle.

It didn't. At the very last second, Gavin leaped out of the way. The large logging truck smashed through the smaller vehicle in a hail of sparks, sending Gavin's crumpled truck through the guardrail and down into the ravine.

Mr. Meacham kept his foot on the gas and they sailed across the bridge and closer to the tree line.

"Almost there!" Pete yelled.

But the truck was done. Something in the engine had given way from the impact, and steam was billowing out from under the hood. The engine sputtered, and the giant vehicle wheezed to a halt.

CHAPTER THIRTY-ONE

Jack slowed his truck as they neared the debris from Gavin's destroyed vehicle. From the embankment, Gavin tried to flag him down. But Jack wasn't going to stop. Assured that his brother was okay, Jack moved past the wreckage and sped up, ignoring Gavin's angry shouts.

On the other side of the bridge, he could see Elliot, Mr. Meacham, and the children standing on the road.

"There they are!" Jack yelled to Grace.

But Grace's attention wasn't on the kids. It was on Elliot. The dragon was moving, rising up onto his hind legs. Elliot stared at the long chain of cars behind Jack and Grace and then, with a gentle nudge, pushed Pete and Natalie behind him protectively.

"Wait . . ." said Grace.

A deep, booming rumble sounded from Elliot's chest. Even from across the bridge, Jack and Grace could see the dragon's eyes turn fierce. He drew in a deep breath. Suddenly, he opened his jaws wide, and a massive jet of flame exploded forth. Elliot was breathing fire! The flame swept across the length of the bridge, all the way toward the last of the convoy of cars.

Jack slammed on the brakes too late, driving straight into the wall of fire. Behind him and Grace, the massive lineup of vehicles screeched to an abrupt halt—most of them driving directly into each other with a series of loud crashes.

From the embankment, Gavin's face turned pale as he watched his brother's truck engulfed in flames.

"Jack . . ." he whispered in horror.

Without hesitation, Gavin sprinted past the pile of cars and straight toward the fire.

CHAPTER THIRTY-TWO

Pete was screaming. "Elliot, stop! Don't hurt them!"

But Elliot couldn't hear him above his own roaring. He was convinced that the people were a threat to Pete, Natalie, and Mr. Meacham. And he wasn't going to let anything hurt them! The dragon continued to breathe a jet of white-hot fire down the length of the bridge. Natalie could barely speak. "My dad . . ." she said, staring at the blaze.

Finally, Elliot stopped. He looked down at the children to make sure they were safe. But their faces—they looked ashen. Why were they upset? Elliot looked back and forth between the children and the bridge, trying to understand.

With the fire extinguished, the smoke began to clear, revealing a huge gap where the wood of the bridge had been burned away. And right on the precipice of the deep, misty ravine was Jack's truck. The front wheels were melted, hanging over open air; the front axle was supported only by charred, crumbling wood. With just one wrong movement, the vehicle would plummet into the deep gorge.

Pete's eyes widened. "Elliot . . ." he pleaded. "You have to fly. You can save them."

Elliot whined softly, uncertain. Those people had tried to hurt him and take Pete away. Why should he help them?

"I know," Pete said, "but . . . not all people are bad. Most people are good. They just don't understand that you can help them."

With a creaking noise, the truck leaned a little farther over the edge of the ravine.

Elliot gently beat his wings, testing them. He winced as his damaged wing stung from the effort. Flying didn't seem to be an option.

* * *

In the car, Grace blinked slowly. She'd hit her head against the dashboard when Jack had slammed on the brakes.

"Grace?" Jack asked. He felt the truck shift forward, his heart leaping into his throat. He threw the truck into reverse. But it was no use; the wheels had no traction.

"It's okay . . . it's okay . . ." he said. "We've just gotta keep still and . . ."

The truck shifted forward again slightly.

Jack's heart was pounding. There was no way for him to get out. His door was already over the edge—if he tried to open it, they would fall. He looked over at Grace. "Can you get out?" he asked.

Grace looked at her door and shook her head. "I don't think so. And I'm not going without you."

Meanwhile, Gavin had reached the back of the truck. But it shifted a little farther and began to slide forward. Instinctively, the logger threw his hands on the bumper, trying to slow the truck's movement. Jack and Grace both cried out in alarm.

"Get out!" Gavin yelled. "Get out of there!"

Jack turned and saw his brother through the back window. He suddenly realized there was another way out. Twisting around, he started to kick at the rear window. The glass shattered. He pushed Grace toward the opening, but it was too late—a horrible groan echoed as the metal and wood shifted and creaked. The truck tipped forward past the point of no return. . . .

Grace grabbed Jack's hand and squeezed it tight.

The truck slid toward the gorge, falling.

CHAPTER THIRTY-THREE

Jack and Grace screamed as the truck began toppling over the edge. But in a split second, the vehicle lurched to a stop.

They opened their eyes. They weren't falling anymore. They weren't moving at all.

They looked up through the front window. There was Elliot! He was standing on the opposite side of the gap in the bridge, holding the truck back from falling with one extended paw. The dragon looked at Jack and Grace and smiled his dragon smile. He began slowly pushing the vehicle backward, away from the gorge and to safety . . . until . . .

The support beams of the bridge crumbled. The truck and the dragon both plummeted into the misty depths below, disappearing in the dark haze.

"NO!" cried Pete and Natalie.

On the other side, the mill workers and the police raced to the edge of the ravine. But there was nothing for anyone to see—only a deep pit and seemingly infinite mist at the bottom.

All was quiet.

Natalie's eyes filled with fresh tears. So did Mr. Meacham's.

"Oh, Grace . . ." Mr. Meacham whispered softly.

Pete stood at the edge of the broken bridge, staring into the empty void below. He refused to believe that his friends were gone.

"C'mon, Elliot," he said to himself.

Pete knelt down at the edge of the abyss. Shock was starting to give way to fear and doubt. Elliot wasn't coming back. The dragon . . . his friend . . . his *family* . . .

"*ELLIOT!*" Pete howled. His voice echoed from the boundless depths below. Mr. Meacham knelt next to him, placing a gentle hand on his shoulder. Several police officers removed their hats and shook their heads sadly, while Gavin could only stare blankly downward in disbelief.

And then there was a noise.

Faint at first. Then louder and louder. A rhythmic thumping, like a heartbeat or . . . wings.

A vision of green rose from the mists in the

ravine. It was Elliot, his wings beating harder than they ever had before! On his back were Grace and Jack, safe and sound!

Everyone cheered! Deputy Smalls stared across the gulf to the other side of the broken bridge as the dragon landed next to Pete. He saw Grace and Jack climbing down from the dragon's back and rushing to hug their loved ones.

The deputy turned to the sheriff. This was certainly something they'd never handled before. "What do we do now, Sheriff?" he asked.

The sheriff shrugged. "Gonna need a new bridge, I guess."

CHAPTER THIRTY-FOUR

Things happened quickly after that. Helicopters approached in the distance. Elliot snorted in concern. He could tell more danger was on its way.

Grace knelt down in front of Pete. She knew there wasn't much time before the floods of people would swarm Elliot and try to figure out what to do with a giant fire-breathing dragon. It was clear he could not stay there. And it was clear he had to move quickly.

She reached into her pocket, finding the compass Pete loved so much. She pressed it into the boy's hand.

"Pete . . ." she said. "Take Elliot. Make sure he's safe. And . . ." She stammered a little, trying to find the words. "And I want you to know that I . . ."

With a deep release of breath, she smiled. "Just know that we're here for you."

Pete felt tears forming at the corners of his eyes. He knew this was good-bye. "Where should we go?" he asked.

Grace pulled Pete close and hugged him.

"Go north," she whispered.

Pete climbed onto the dragon's soft fur, and Elliot began to beat his wings. As Natalie, Grace, Jack, and the rest of the crowd watched, the pair launched into the air. The bright sun sunk low on the horizon, streaking the sky with gold and red.

Pete looked out across the expanse of forest below and up into the limitless sky.

It was good to be back in the forest. Back with his friend.

And for the moment, that was all that mattered.

Elliot flew for a long while. Eventually, the dragon landed in the deep shadows of one of the innermost parts of the woods, touching ground at the base of the tree fort. But it was not the sanctuary it had once been; the wreckage of the destroyed tree house lay scattered across the forest floor.

Elliot sighed, and Pete wandered through the debris.

"We can't stay here," Pete said.

Elliot made a sympathetic cooing sound. He understood.

"People will come looking for you. They know you're here," Pete continued.

Elliot nodded solemnly. That was true. In an attempt to lighten the mood, he disappeared, reappearing a few feet from where he had been.

Pete laughed.

"I can't disappear, though," he said.

Elliot camouflaged himself again. Something came rustling across the ground, pushed by an invisible force, as if by magic.

It was the storybook *Elliot Gets Lost*.

Pete picked up the book, staring at it. He flipped it open, and there, on the first page, was a handwritten inscription. Something he'd long overlooked.

To Pete, it said. *Love, Mommy and Daddy.*

Pete stared at the inscription for a long time, then finally looked up. Elliot materialized, making a reassuring grunt. The dragon nodded his head at the boy as if prompting him to turn the pages.

The final page of the book showed an image

of the little puppy reunited with his family. Pete remembered Jack reading that part of the story only the night before and how at peace he'd felt sitting there with Jack, Grace, and Natalie. He understood what Elliot was trying to tell him.

Tears filled Pete's eyes. "But I don't want to leave you," he said.

The dragon smiled, and then he made the most reassuring noise a dragon could ever make—a deep, comforting purr. He knew it was going to be okay . . . for both of them.

The little boy threw his arms around the dragon, holding him tight, his tears wetting Elliot's fur. They stood that way for a long time, as the last embers of daylight faded and the forest fell into darkness.

Pete looked up—far above, into the sky. The North Star twinkled in the darkness. It was time to go.

CHAPTER THIRTY-FIVE

The sun had started to rise. It had been a long night of answering questions and filling out police reports. Now Grace drove her jeep down the road, heading back toward town. She glanced up, seeing the last trace of the North Star fading in the morning light. Jack sat in the passenger seat beside her, while in the backseat, Natalie had fallen sound asleep.

Jack took Grace's hand and gave her a reassuring smile as they pulled up in front of the house. Suddenly, their eyes grew wide.

There, on the lawn, was Pete.

Grace leaped out of the jeep and ran to Pete as fast as she could, throwing her arms around the little boy. He hugged her back tightly.

A familiar sound filled the air: the reverberation of large beating wings. As they looked up, the echo faded away.

Hand in hand, Grace and Pete walked up to the front door, Jack and Natalie at their sides. They headed into the house—a new family.

As Pete turned to cast one more look out on the horizon, he smiled, remembering all that had been and looking forward to all that would be.

* * *

Some time later, the town of Millhaven was back to normal. Folks hurried up and down the main street. Kids rode their bikes to school. And just beyond the hustle and bustle of the forest mill, a new sight rose: freshly-planted trees, growing beautiful and tall and green.

It was as though there had never been any excitement of a secret dragon living in the forest at all. In fact, if you asked folks around town, most of them would say it was just a story.

But there was one little boy who knew that it was all true.

And he was off on another adventure.

The sun glinted off of Jack's jeep as he, Grace, Pete, and Natalie drove north. Pete's hair was now neatly trimmed, and he wore properly-fitting clothes. But the old forest-boy spark still gleamed in his eye. Ahead of them in the distance, snow-capped mountains loomed. That's where they were headed.

Together, the family reached the base of the mountains and began the long trek upward. Up, up, up, well beyond any marked trail. Pete led the way, pushing forward until, finally, they reached the crest of a mountaintop valley.

And that's where Pete waited. He scanned the tall, waving grass, searching. He knew he must be here . . .

Suddenly, a low, friendly growl purred behind him.

Pete turned. He whooped with joy.

It was Elliot!

Pete hugged his friend tearfully. They were reunited once more!

Grace beamed as she watched Pete and Elliot play together. The boy and dragon leaped and tumbled just like old times.

And then, Pete ran right off the precipice of the mountain plateau. Of course, Elliot swooped down to catch him. But what happened next made everyone's eyes grow wide with wonder.

An entire flock of dragons suddenly soared up next to Elliot, flying alongside him.

Elliot had found his family after all, high in the mountains of the North!

Pete buried his face in Elliot's fur, and the dragon smiled. Elliot was overwhelmed with happiness. Happiness at finding a family. Happiness at finding a home. But mostly, happiness at being together with his friend again.

Elliot would always be Pete's dragon. And that made him happiest of all.